The job posting said nothin[...]
Nor did it mention qualifi[...]
speeding bullet and be able to leap tall buildings in a single bound. So Cassandra figured they weren't looking for superheroes. Let's just say the only running she ever did was when she was running late, and her leaping was limited to conclusions—like when she assumed 'til death do us part really meant death and not just until some double-D, twenty-something bimbo came along.

Cassandra figured this particular job involved soliciting for a green charity. Ever since Al Gore won an Oscar back in 2007, people had been jumping on the green bandwagon. She was all in favor of saving the planet, but her environmental concerns came second to her need for a job with benefits—green or otherwise.

Novellas and Novelettes
Elementary, My Dear Gertie
Moms in Black, A Mom Squad Caper
Once Upon a Romance
Finding Mr. Right

Children's Chapter Book
The Magic Paintbrush

Nonfiction
Top Ten Reasons Your Novel is Rejected
House Unauthorized
Bake, Love, Write
We'd Rather Be Writing

Moms in Black
A Mom Squad Caper

LOIS WINSTON

Author's Note

This novella was originally published as *Mom Squad* in conjunction with author CJ Lyons' Shadow Ops series and was part of the now-defunct Kindle Worlds program. It has since been revised to remove all connections to that series, expanded, and republished with the express permission of author CJ Lyons.

Cover design by L. Winston

ISBN:978-1-940795-53-9

DEDICATION

To all the brave souls who put their lives on the line every day to keep us safe.

ACKNOWLEDGMENTS

To Dustin Dodd, bomb squad member, for educating me about some really nasty stuff. Thank you for doing what you do. May you always remain safe.

To Donnell Bell and Irene Peterson for once again wielding their computerized red pencils to help me perfect this book.

ONE

Some people retire from government service with a pat on the back, a commendation for a job well done, and a hefty pension. Others are forced out when an operation goes south and the politicians demand a sacrificial lamb. Forget all the accomplishments of the past, the bad actors brought down, the lives saved.

Forget the fact that she had pointed out the flaws in the operation from the moment of its ill-conceived conception, had waved a myriad of red flags, highlighting everything that could—and eventually did—go wrong. In the end, she became the target of all those bureaucrats, politicians, and political appointees who had refused to listen to her expert advice. The people in power needed someone to blame—someone other than themselves and their cohorts, someone not a member of The Old Boys' Club—even though many of them owed their lives to her.

At least her teams had understood, even though they'd also been forced out in undeserved disgrace when everything she'd spent a lifetime creating had been flushed out of existence. However, the private sector had already snapped up most of those dedicated men and women and for salaries that more than compensated for the loss of a government pension. Those still unemployed were weighing the pros and cons of various offers. Everyone would bounce back.

Everyone but her.

After thirty years of government service, the only options Carla Jordan now weighed were the monumental decision of whether to take up gardening or pottery. Heck, with so much time now on her hands, she could do both, as well as join a yoga class, a book club, and whatever else retirees did to kill eight or ten or twelve or twenty-four hours a day.

What she hadn't considered having to weigh was whether or not to invite into her home the government official currently standing on her doorstep. It had come as quite a surprise when she checked her security camera and discovered Anthony Granville, the newly confirmed Attorney General, standing on her front porch. Her first inclination was to slam the door in his face, but three decades of counter-intelligence work had trained her to hide all emotion.

Forget hiding emotion. If nothing else, forced retirement should allow her to express her bitterness and anger over the way she and her teams had been treated. People who put their lives on the line each day to protect the country shouldn't have to worry about being used as pawns in a political tug-a-war. Or worse yet, thrown under the bus by congressmen who put their careers and reelection bids ahead of the safety of the citizens who paid their salaries. But that's exactly what had happened.

She squared her shoulders and lifted her chin before swinging the door open. Without preamble she asked, "Am I about to receive my long-overdue apology?"

"If it were up to me, Carla, I'd put you in charge of Homeland Security."

Well, that certainly took her by surprise!

"So why are you here, Tony?" asked Edward, coming up behind her.

"To twist your wife's arm, pick her brains, and make her an offer she can't refuse. You, too, Ed."

Carla crossed her arms over her chest and raised her chin in defiance. After what the government had put her and her people through, did Tony really have the balls to expect her to forgive and forget? "I'm not coming back, not in any capacity. I've had my fill of you government bozos."

He pulled an exaggerated frown. "Even me?"

No, she couldn't lump Tony in with the rest of them. He'd been one of the few to come to her defense when a powerful senator had railroaded her in a bid to save his own neck. He'd pushed for her indictment on trumped up charges that could have led to her serving a lengthy prison term.

Carla had fought back, exposing his corruption. Now that senator and his partner-in-crime spent their days decked out in orange jumpsuits instead of the taxpayer-funded three-thousand-dollar bespoke suits they'd once worn. Justice had won out but at a price that had soured Carla to her previous life. She was through with government service. Now and forever.

She offered Tony a begrudging nod. "Present company excluded."

"Glad to hear that. Now let me tell you what I have in mind. Then if you still want to kick me the hell out, I'll bend over and offer you a wide target."

Carla softened her stance and waved Tony into the living room. "You have five minutes."

"Fair enough." He glanced at the furniture, unable to mask the shock registering on his face.

"Not the décor you expected from a hard-ass warrior like me?" she asked.

To his credit Granville shook his head and chuckled as he settled into the middle of her floral upholstered sofa with its overabundance of coordinated toss pillows. "Definitely not. I would have expected hard-lined minimalism. You're a woman of many talents, Carla Jordan. And even more surprises."

"He definitely wants something," Carla stage-whispered to Edward as they each opted for one of the two deep rose overstuffed tufted armchairs separated from the sofa by a white shabby chic coffee table.

Edward nodded as he tapped the face of his watch. "Clock's ticking, Granville."

Tony leaned forward, his elbows resting on his knees. "Carla and her department made tremendous headway in eliminating threats from overseas terrorist organizations looking to strike on American soil."

Edward turned to his wife. "I think that was the thank-you we've been waiting to hear."

She shrugged. "I'm not sure you could call it an apology, but at least it's an acknowledgment."

Granville grimaced before continuing, "The president, along with Homeland Security and our various other counter-intelligence organizations, believes our greatest security threats right now are from right-wing militias and radicalized lone wolves, not various foreign Jihadist groups."

"Not an illogical conclusion, given the recent attacks across the country and the numerous arrests of various sympathizers," said Carla. She locked eyes with Granville. "Including a certain senator and congressman."

To Granville's credit, he accepted the dagger she hurled without offering up any defense of the government's campaign to go along with the two traitors as they tried to convince everyone of Carla's malfeasance in order to cover up their own treason.

"You'd go a long way in stopping the fomenters and perpetrators by shutting down their social media accounts," said Edward.

Granville heaved a sigh as he ran his hands through his buzz cut. "We've tried. Some of the social media sites are working with us; others refuse, citing first amendment rights. However, even when we do get compliance, new accounts immediately pop up. There are tens of thousands of them. It's like a never-ending game of Whack-a-Mole. On top of that, we've now discovered many terrorist organizations are using encrypted end-to-end smart phone programs to prevent us from accessing their communications once they lure in new recruits."

Carla cut to the chase. "What does this have to do with us?"

"I'm getting to that. As you know, some of our intelligence gathering operations, especially those by the NSA, have been severely hampered or even curtailed of late. Too many citizens object to the government snooping into their lives, and disgruntled voters tend to kick their representatives out of Congress come election time. Above all else, even the safety of the nation, congressmen and senators want to keep their jobs."

Carla raised both eyebrows. "Oh, really? Tell us something we don't know, Tony."

Granville heaved a more forceful sigh. "I did fight for you."

"And yet here we are," said Carla, extending both arms in a wide sweep.

He grimaced but plowed forward. "I have an idea for putting a serious dent in terrorist recruitment operations."

"And how does that concern us?" asked Carla.

Granville laid out his plan. He concluded by adding, "You'd sit at the top of the pyramid, directing and coordinating the various satellite groups. Each group would consist of eight teams with one person heading each group. The group leaders report directly to you."

"Then what?" asked Edward.

"When a threat is identified, I notify the proper authorities who take over and neutralize the threat."

"Those proper authorities didn't exactly do a bang-up job in the past," said Edward. "That's why Carla's department was created in the first place."

"We've learned from our mistakes," said Granville. "Communications between various agencies are improving all the time."

Edward snorted. "Forgive my skepticism."

Carla eyed Granville as she mulled over his proposition. He had offered her a Karmic, stick-it-to-the-man do-over to avenge the wrong dealt her by the government she'd sworn to protect. Granted, few people would ever know of her role in this new operation, but few people had known about her previous role—until treason had trumped patriotism in the hallowed halls of the capitol and her picture was plastered across every news outlet in the country.

She glanced over at Edward. He offered her a nod that told her he knew what she was thinking and would go along with whatever decision she made.

"We have no feet on the ground?" she asked.

Granville patted the sofa cushion. "You and Edward remain safe in your chintz-covered ivory tower."

Carla laughed at the absurdity of his plan. "And Congress is onboard with this?"

"Congress won't even know you exist."

"Congress holds the purse strings," said Edward. "How the hell do you plan to pay for this operation without their approval?"

Granville smiled. "Through a private donor."

"He'd have to have incredibly deep pockets," said Carla.

"The deepest."

Carla studied Tony as she mentally catalogued everything she knew about him. Then it hit her. She smiled back. "Liam Hatch."

"Give that lady a cigar. You haven't lost your touch, Carla."

"How do you plan to recruit your team members?" asked Edward.

"That's the genius part," said Tony. "There are thousands of ordinary citizens across the country who have lost family members to terrorism. They want justice but have no way of achieving it on their own. We're going to offer them the opportunity to make a difference and gain justice for their loved ones."

Including Granville. This idea of his was too personal. Carla jumped to her feet. "You want to use untrained civilians? You're out of your freaking mind, Tony. There are only a million different ways this plan could blow up in your face."

Edward reached for her hand and nudged her back into her chair. "Actually, I think he may have something here. With the proper training this could work."

Carla stared at him. Edward might be ex-special forces, but he was the gadget loving techno-geek, who'd employed his vast knowledge of computers to wage war on terrorists. She preferred more old-fashioned methods, like color-coded pins in a map that spanned the width of a wall, to keep her abreast of both her teams and all worldwide threats. What Tony Granville had proposed was more in Edward's wheelhouse than hers.

Carla mulled over Granville's plan. She always trusted her gut, and her gut had always before told her not to trust civilians. They were too unpredictable. Too many things could go wrong, things that this time could land her in prison. Or worse.

Edward was far more analytical. Their eyes met, and he nodded again. He actually thought this crazy idea of Granville's could work. Maybe it could—but not without some serious modifications.

"I get to pick the group leaders," she finally said. "And they won't be civilians. I want trained operatives in charge of each of the satellite facilities."

"Fair enough," said Granville. "As long as Gavin Demarco heads up one of the satellites."

She knew Demarco and why Granville would want him in the game. Fine. The guy was FBI. He'd know the difference between revenge and justice. At least she hoped so. "Demarco know about this?"

"We came up with the idea together."

Given their connection, this didn't surprise her. She nodded. "Fine."

Granville stood and extended his hand. Carla accepted it, matching his solid handshake with her own equally firm grip.

Edward clapped his hands together, then rose from his chair. He looped an arm around Carla and slapped Granville on the back. "Looks like we're getting the band back together."

TWO

Six months later

Tired of all the problems?
Be part of the solution.
Full and part-time positions available. Flex hours. Full benefits.
Ideal position for moms reentering the workforce. Apply at
www.savingtheworld.us

The job posting that popped up in her email said nothing about wearing spandex and a cape. Nor did it mention qualified applicants must be faster than a speeding bullet and be able to leap tall buildings in a single bound. So Cassandra figured they weren't looking for superheroes. Let's just say the only running she ever did was when she was running late, and her leaping was limited to conclusions—like when she assumed 'til death do us part really meant death and not just until some double-D, twenty-something bimbo came along.

Cassandra figured this particular job involved soliciting for a green charity. Ever since Al Gore won an Oscar back in 2007, people had been jumping on the green bandwagon. She was all in favor of saving the planet, but her environmental concerns came second to her need for a job with benefits—green or otherwise.

Although her current position as Arts and Entertainment reporter for the local paper afforded her flexible working hours, the only benefit she received was free concert and theater tickets—as long as she covered the event. Short of stripping or pole dancing, she'd do just about anything for free health insurance, including telemarketing calls or going door-to-door collecting signatures for petitions.

The only other position she'd found so far that included flexible hours and health benefits was pulling shots at Starbucks, but they had a waiting list for all their local coffee shops, and she wasn't about to trek into Manhattan to work as a barista.

Living in the suburbs meant spending part of each day as the family chauffeur. One parent. Two kids involved in multiple extra-curricular activities. Scratch any jobs in Manhattan.

Since she'd registered at several job sites, she figured the email was legit, but still, she took precautions. The last thing she needed was to infect her computer with some malware or a virus too new for her protection software to catch.

She hovered her curser over the link. The same URL popped up. A good sign but not necessarily proof of legitimacy. Instead of clicking on the link, she typed the website into her browser and hit ENTER.

To her surprise, the site contained nothing other than a brief application form requesting name, age, phone number, and level of education. She figured employers didn't need to know much about their employees if the job only entailed making cold calls or knocking on doors to solicit signatures and donations. However, she would have liked to know the who-what-where-when-and-how concerning savingtheworld.us. She tried a Google search of the organization, but the only site that popped up was the one with the application.

Once upon a time Cassandra might have thought twice about sending off any personal information into cyberspace, but since the site wasn't asking for a Social Security number and all the other information was already available to anyone clicking around the Internet, she figured, what the hell?

The Ex had knocked up his latest Double-D Bimbo, who was now carrying his twin bimbettes. He'd dropped his own kids and Cassandra from his health insurance (in direct violation of the divorce decree), married the Double-D Bimbo, and added her to his policy.

Cassandra was in the process of hauling his slimy ass into court over that, but since The Ex was now also three months behind in child support, she knew she had to become more proactive in order to protect her kids and herself. Those extra-curricular activities included too many sports. And sports went hand-in-hand with periodic visits to the emergency room. Without health insurance one broken arm could put her in debt up the yin-yang.

She crossed her fingers, hoping she wasn't getting snookered by some Nigerian scam artist "prince", took a deep breath, and filled in the boxes with the necessary information.

NAME: Cassandra Davenport
AGE: 38
PHONE NUMBER: 908-555-1234

LEVEL OF EDUCATION: college graduate

Before she had second thoughts, she hit SEND.

~*~

Two hours later, while she was in the middle of snaking a clogged toilet—snake in one hand, how-to plumbing book in the other (yet another task she'd had to assume, thanks to The Ex and Double-D, because she could no longer afford to call a plumber)— the phone rang.

"Cassandra Davenport?"

"Yes?"

"I'm calling from savingtheworld.us. We'd like you to come in for an interview tomorrow."

Cassandra dropped the snake and scrambled for a pencil and paper as the caller rattled off the designated time and an address in Newark.

Newark?

Definitely not a prime New Jersey location for much of anything other than drug deals and flying bullets, no matter what the PR flacks would have you believe about a Newark Renaissance. Exactly how legit was savingtheworld.us? Benefits or no benefits, she wasn't about to risk her life or freedom by becoming a drug mule for cocaine traffickers. Then again, how many Columbian drug lords offered health insurance? "Is the job located at that address?" she asked.

"No."

The caller hung up before Cassandra could ask another question.

~*~

The next morning after dropping Cooper and Hayley at school,

Cassandra edged her car into rush hour traffic on the Garden State Parkway, otherwise known as the Garden State Parking Lot. The address she'd been given turned out to be the DoubleTree Hotel near Penn Station. Why didn't the caller just say that?

The fourteen-mile trip took forty minutes, which made Cassandra ten minutes late by the time she found a spot in the hotel parking lot and hustled up to the second-floor conference room where the interview was to take place.

Nothing like making a great first impression!

"Traffic on the Parkway?" asked a woman standing at a table outside the room.

Cassandra hadn't yet given her name to the woman. How the hell did she know which road she'd taken? Or even that she'd driven? She could just as easily have arrived via NJTransit.

Dumbfounded, all Cassandra could do was nod. The woman wore black head-to-toe—a black silk shirt paired with a black pencil skirt, black stockings, black heels. Even her glasses were black rimmed. But despite the New York sophistication of the outfit, the woman standing behind the reception table was rather nondescript, average height and weight with shoulder-length dark brown hair. The kind of woman you'd see pushing a cart down the aisles of Trader Joe's or chairing a PTA committee meeting.

Me in black.

Right down to the shoulder-length dark brown hair and brown eyes.

Before Cassandra could say anything, the woman ushered her into the conference room.

Another woman, also dressed completely in black and also looking like your average suburban housewife, greeted Cassandra inside the room and led her to a seat, one of those chairs with built-in desks, like the ones she remembered from high school. A laptop sat on the desk. "Please follow the instructions on the computer screen, Ms. Davenport."

"How did—?"

"No talking, please."

Cassandra carefully squeezed into the seat, placing one hand on the laptop to prevent it from toppling off as the desk fought against the intrusion of her body. At five-foot-four and a hundred-twenty pounds, she was hardly gargantuan, but she suddenly felt like Gulliver in Lilliput. Forget high school. These chairs had to be surplus from an old junior high school renovation.

She glanced around the room. About a dozen other women, all appearing to be in their thirties and forties, filled most of the remaining seats. No men. Some of the women stared at the computer screen in front of them; others clicked away at the keyboards. All looked extremely uncomfortable.

Cassandra lifted the lid of her computer. The screen glowed to life with a personal greeting:

Welcome, Ms. Davenport. Please answer all the questions in as little time as possible. Do not skip any questions. Press ENTER when you're ready to begin.

She pressed ENTER. One question popped up.

Would you rather be:
( ) a CIA agent
( ) a dermatologist
( ) a CPA

There was no OTHER option. None of the answers appealed to her. Not even remotely. She didn't do guns. The idea of spending her days dealing with eczema, acne, and melanomas grossed her out. And her inability to balance her own checkbook eliminated the possibility of handling someone else's business accounts.

Besides, what did any of these selections have to do with saving the world? Was this a CIA recruitment session in disguise? Or was savingtheworld.us looking for number crunchers? Perhaps, recruits to work in leprosy colonies? Did leprosy colonies even still exist? She had no idea. Given her limited options, she chose the lesser of three evils.

(X) CIA agent

As long as I don't have to handle a gun. But there was no space to add any explanations or disclaimers, so she clicked to the next page.

Would you rather be:
( ) a commercial fisherman
( ) a mathematics professor
( ) a nail salon owner

It dawned on Cassandra that she was taking some form of a Myers-Briggs personality test. She hadn't taken one of those since the one that matched her up with her college roommate more than twenty years ago. The results couldn't have been further off base. No two people were ever more mismatched than the perpetually stoned Cannabis Queen of Jamaica, Queens and the former teenage Goody Two-Shoes Cassandra Anne Davenport. Luckily, the pothead dropped out of school before Thanksgiving break.

Getting back to the farmer, the professor, and the salon owner (which sounded either like the beginning of a walk-into-a-bar joke or a casting call for the reality TV version of *Gilligan's Island*,) she once again clicked on the lesser of three evils.

Hell, at least I'll have great looking nails.

After ten more equally ridiculous questions, both carpal tunnel syndrome and a stiff neck began to creep up on her, thanks to the less-than-ergonomic conditions. The schoolroom type chairs, not only designed by some clueless idiot who assumed everyone on the planet was right-handed, but created decades before laptops were invented, began to feel like something Torquemada might have used as part of a torture session during the Spanish Inquisition.

An image of Will Smith in the egg chair from *Men in Black* flashed across her mind. Never let it be said that Cassandra Davenport ran with the lemmings. Channeling her inner Will Smith, she stood up, grabbed the laptop, and made her way to the perimeter of the room where she settled onto the floor, her back propped against the wall, the laptop perched on her lap. The woman in black proctor raised an eyebrow but said nothing.

Cassandra went on to the next set of questions, which dealt with personal likes and dislikes. All were as ridiculous as the occupation questions:

Would you rather watch:
( ) *Survivor*
( ) *The Young and the Restless*

( ) *Dog the Bounty Hunter*

They had to be kidding! Since she'd never watched any of the shows listed, she resorted to the eenie-meenie-minie-moe method. *Dog the Bounty Hunter* (whatever that was) won out by default.

The remainder of the five hundred questions were equally as ridiculous. Although the more questions she answered, the more inquisitive she became about the who-what-where-when-and-how of savingtheworld.us.

As she worked, she noticed many of the women close their computers and leave by the door through which she'd entered. When Cassandra completed the last piece of nonsense, a question asking her to choose between sleeping on a soft, medium, or firm mattress—she chose firm—a new message popped up on her screen:

Thank you, Ms. Davenport. Please take the laptop and proceed through the double-doors at the back of the room.

Cassandra hadn't seen anyone else go through those doors, and only three other women remained in the room along with her. As she scanned the room, another woman closed her laptop, left it on the chair-desk, and exited through the main doors. She glanced over at the woman in black who pointed to the back of the room—as if she could read Cassandra's mind. Shades of *Twilight Zone*!

This entire experience seemed way too woo-woo for a non-profit organization. After about the twentieth question she'd come to the conclusion that savingtheworld.us had little to do with greenhouse gases or global warming. The truth probably lay on the other side of that door. If nothing else, savingtheworld.us had piqued her curiosity. So she closed the lid, cradled the laptop under her arm, and strode toward the back of the room. Cassandra was a woman on a mission. Whether she was offered a job or not, she wanted answers.

Boy, did she get them!

THREE

Be careful what you wish for. To say Cassandra was unprepared for the answers to her questions was the understatement of the universe. At least the Universe According to Cassandra Davenport.

The door she entered led into a service corridor where she found another woman in black waiting for her. "Follow me, Ms. Davenport."

Cassandra didn't bother saying anything. From prior experience with the women in black, she knew she wouldn't get any answers, so she refrained from asking how the woman knew her name.

Instead, she played the good girl, nodded, and followed alongside her. The woman led her to another door at the far end of the corridor and ushered her inside a smaller conference room. This one contained the requisite conference table and chairs. A man and two more women in black, both on the cusp of middle age, sat at the head of the table, the man in the center, the women flanking him on either side.

The man rose when she entered. "Welcome, Ms. Davenport. Please have a seat."

Cassandra placed the laptop on the conference table and settled into the chair nearest the door. "Okay, let's cut to the chase here. Why all the cloak and dagger?"

She never was one for pussyfooting. She hated games. If she were being coarse—which she usually wasn't since she had to set an example for her kids and Lord knows, their father certainly hadn't—she'd say, *Shit or Get Off the Pot* was her motto of choice.

The man grinned. "Direct. I like that." He glanced from side to side to ascertain the reaction of his companions. Both nodded in agreement but neither grinned. Their expressions remained...expressionless. "I think we're all going to work together very well," he said.

Did this mean he was going to offer her a job? But doing what? She continued with the direct approach. "And exactly what type of work do you do?"

"Very important work, Ms. Davenport. Work that is of the highest priority for the well-being of our country and its citizens."

"So you are CIA."

He raised an eyebrow. "Where did you get that idea?"

"From the first question on the computer. And even though there was no place to add any qualifiers to the answers I chose, I'm telling you right now, I don't do guns. Or any other form of deadly weaponry."

"We're not CIA, Ms. Davenport."

"Oh." She stared at him. His face had taken on a serious look, almost a deadly look, but she couldn't help but notice the undercurrent of sexuality he exuded. The guy was hot. Latin lover type hot. She wouldn't be surprised to find that parts of his gene pool originally hailed from south of the border or the Iberian Peninsula. His was the kind of hot that could have placed him on a Calvin Klein billboard.

Weren't government agents supposed to blend into the crowd? No way would this guy ever blend in anywhere. "Well, it's pretty clear you're not just some environmental organization looking for clerks, fundraisers, or petition gatherers," she said. "So exactly what is www.savingtheworld.us? And for that matter, who are you?"

A hint of humor passed across his face. "I was about to get to that."

Cassandra leaned back in her chair and crossed her arms over her chest. "I'm listening." It occurred to her that she'd unleashed her inner bitch. She needed a position with flexible hours and benefits. Yet here she was doing her damnedest to sabotage her chances of getting a job that didn't involve asking, "Tall, grande, or venti?" She chalked it up to spending the last few hours answering those inane computer questions.

"My name is Gavin Demarco," he said.

Score two points for her powers of observation. Latino genes. At least on his father's side. Irish on his mother's? Gavin certainly wasn't a Latino name, and that deep green gaze that was currently boring into her had to come from somewhere other than Central or South America. But why did she care? *Concentrate on the job interview, Cassandra!*

"And these are my associates, Hanna Bereket and Noreen Jones." He nodded first to his left, then his right.

Hanna had an olive complexion that spoke of possible Middle Eastern or Indian heritage. She wore her ebony hair pulled into a sleek, tight bun at the base of her neck. The laugh lines around her eyes and mouth told Cassandra she didn't always wear such a solemn expression.

Noreen was a slightly thinner, light-skinned black woman with a smattering of freckles across the bridge of her nose. She wore her chestnut curly hair pulled back in a loose ponytail. Both women appeared to be about five or six years older than Cassandra. Although neither possessed Victoria's Secret bodies, they both looked like they worked out, something Cassandra hadn't done since high school—as evidenced by the slight muffin top and underarm jiggle she'd noticed the last time she stood semi-naked in front of her mirror.

"If you choose to join us," continued Demarco, "the three of you will be working together as a team, reporting directly to me."

"Doing?"

This time Cassandra caught a quick upturn of the mouth from both Hanna and Noreen as well as Demarco. "As I said, we're not CIA. We're not part of any official government organization."

"There are *unofficial* government organizations?"

"We fall into that category."

*Men (*or *Women*, in this case*) in Black* meets *Alias*?

"We live in troubling times, Ms. Davenport. The world changed on September 11, 2001 and has continued to grow darker and more dangerous with each passing year."

"Tell me something I don't know, Mr. Demarco." The day the towers fell she'd lost both her father and brother, two of the many first responder casualties of that day.

Demarco continued, "With what's going on in the world, the intelligence community and law enforcement are stretched beyond thin. Besides that, we've discovered that there are certain aspects of the fight against terrorism that lend themselves better to non-traditional investigative measures, where conventional agency bureaucracy and procedures often hamper, rather than aid in the prevention of attacks and apprehension of suspected terrorists."

"So which government agency are you with?"

"None."

None? Something was beginning to sound rather questionable about Demarco and his women in black. "Are you a vigilante group?"

"Hardly. We're sanctioned by the government."

"But you're not *part* of the government?"

"That's correct. We're a private organization that reports directly to the Attorney General of the United States."

"You're general contractors?"

"In a manner of speaking, but we're not paid by the government for our services. This enables us to remain under the radar, bypassing congressional scrutiny."

"So how do you get paid?"

"We're funded by a grant from the private sector."

"This is legal?"

"Perfectly legal. Those on a need-to-know basis within the government are kept well apprised of our activities. When we identify a threat, the Attorney General is immediately notified, and he mobilizes the proper government agencies to neutralize the situation."

"I'm hardly spy material, Mr. Demarco." Hell, she never even read any Nancy Drew books as a kid.

"*Spy* is such a negative word, Ms. Davenport. We perform counter-intelligence work. We're detectives. Just a bit unorthodox in our methods."

"Meaning illegal? The sort of thing that some say goes on at Guantanamo?"

"I've never been to Guantanamo."

"You didn't answer my question."

"We're committed to protecting the citizens of this country."

She noted that he sidestepped the question. She decided not to press. "Then why aren't you www.savingthecountry.us?"

"The website was taken." He said this with such a deadpan expression that Cassandra didn't know whether he was joking or serious. "We skim the scum off the pond of humanity," he continued, "one terrorist at a time, making the world a safer place for everyone. What we do is important work."

If what he said was true, she knew a deadbeat dad she'd like to sic these guys on.

Noreen spoke for the first time. "We're the good guys, Ms. Davenport."

"And we want you to join us," added Hanna.

Cassandra shook her head. "I don't see how someone like me is suited for counter-intelligence work. Exactly where do I fit into all this? Why me? I'm a suburban housewife who covers the arts and entertainment scene for a local newspaper. How am I remotely qualified to fight any sort of crime?" *And it better not be with a gun.*

"We were housewives, too," said Hanna with a nod in Noreen's direction. "Now we kick butt."

"Metaphorically speaking," added Hanna with a wink.

"Women, especially mothers," said Demarco, "have skill sets that lend themselves to our work. You're phenomenal at multitasking and problem solving."

"Men are incapable of multitasking," said Hanna. "Or at least multitasking with any amount of success. Surely you've noticed that."

"Definitely." The only multitasking The Ex was capable of was lying and cheating at the same time. Cassandra glanced at Demarco, expecting him to take offense to Hanna's statement, but he nodded in agreement.

"The last few years have proven to us that the type of intense training operatives receive in the armed forces and places like Quantico might work well for certain situations but not others," he said. "The alphabet agencies are often hamstrung, forced to play by certain rules. The bad guys play by no rules. We," he indicated his companions with a sweep of his hands, "are attempting to level the playing field."

His explanation made no sense to Cassandra, but then again, little of the day so far had made any sense to her. "How does a quasi-legitimate group of housewives give our country any leverage against crime and terrorism?"

"You'd be surprised," he said. "I'm former FBI. We're very focused thinkers. Too focused at times. We don't always see the subtle nuances the way your average problem-solving mom does."

"We blend into the background," said Noreen. "After a certain age women become invisible. If you're not twenty-something and thin as a rail, no one notices you. We're not memorable. We use that to our advantage."

Cassandra could see the advantages of having a broad spectrum of ethnicities working to thwart terrorism. She'd blend into the woodwork in some places, Noreen and Hanna in others.

"I give these two complete freedom and base my course of action on their input," said Demarco.

"So you're the one with the gun? The brawn to their brains?" she asked.

"I call the shots. Hanna and Noreen—and you, if you join us—along with my other teams, are the out-of-the-box thinkers who present me with the options needed to catch the bad guys. Sometimes each team operates independently. Other times, in groups."

"No guns?"

"We'll discuss that later."

"I don't do guns."

"I heard you the first time."

"What makes you so sure I'm the right person for this job? The closest I've ever come to law enforcement is watching *Law & Order* reruns while I'm folding laundry."

"For one thing, you were the only person who passed the chair test," said Hanna with a nod to a television screen mounted on the wall to Cassandra's left. It showed the now-empty room where the test had taken place.

"An idea you copped from *Men in Black*," she said.

"Whatever works," said Demarco with a shrug. "Noreen came up with that idea."

"Anyone could have done what I did," said Cassandra.

"But you were the only one with the guts to do it," said Hanna. "And even after you moved to the floor, no one else followed you."

"You also rated superior on the computer test," said Noreen.

"A totally bogus test and you all know it," she said. "How about being honest with me?"

"See, this is why you're so qualified for the job," said Demarco. "You saw through all the bullshit. You're right, Ms. Davenport. We knew we wanted you before today. We did our homework."

Cassandra squelched a gasp. "You've been spying on me?"

"Doing our job. Detective work. We delved into your background and found we liked what we saw."

"Then why all this phony crap?" she asked. "The chairs. The test. The other women in black. Who are they?"

"Parts of other teams," said Demarco. "And today's little theatrics were to make sure we weren't making a mistake about you or any of the other women we've chosen. As well as the ones we didn't."

"All the other women left by the main door," she said. "I was the only one who was told to use the back door."

"In your group. The interviews are ongoing. You proved to us that we didn't make a mistake in our initial assessment of you. We want you, Ms. Davenport. I want you."

Cassandra noted those sultry forest green eyes of his were once again boring into her. *Put like that, how could a girl resist?* Then she quickly added to herself, *Are you out of your freaking mind, Cassandra Davenport?*

Gavin Demarco began to enumerate what he'd discovered about her. He and his Mom Squad, as she was told they called themselves, had done their homework. In less than two hours— between the time she filled out their brief questionnaire on the computer and the call that came while she snaked the toilet— they'd learned more about her than she knew about herself. Big Brother had definitely taken over cyberspace.

Or had they? What if that, too, wasn't the truth? What if they'd been spying on her for days? Weeks? "How'd you learn so much about me in such a short period of time?" she asked.

"We have quite a few resources at our disposal," he said.

To say she was impressed would be the understatement of all

understatements. They'd even uncovered her IQ. *She* didn't know her IQ score! "So what is it?" she asked, unable to suppress her curiosity.

"Five points into genius range," said Noreen.

She had no idea she was that bright. Then again, she'd aced just about every test she'd ever taken in school and graduated Summa Cum Laude, but she'd always attributed that to a strong work ethic and lots of studying. Now two decades later, she discovers she could have studied less, partied more, and still gotten great grades. *Damn! Where's the justice?*

What interested Demarco and his group in her was a combination of things that all added up to her fitting a specific profile. And she'd always thought she was just your average caring person with a moderate amount of smarts. He saw her in a completely different light, as someone with a hell of a lot of untapped potential. Or so he said.

"Why did you give up social work?" he asked.

She had a feeling with all the research he and his team had done, they already knew the answer to this question, but she supposed they wanted to hear it directly from her. "I burned out. Like just about every other social worker in this country. Too many cases, not enough time in the day, and a system that worked against us. Social service agencies are more concerned with paperwork than people. When I got pregnant, I had an excuse to stop beating my brains against a bureaucratic brick wall."

She paused for a moment and eyed each of them. "In other words, I copped out. I'm not proud of that. I wanted to help people in need. I failed.

"So now I write up reviews of community theater productions and concerts at the various performing arts venues around the state and would continue doing so—"

"If you didn't need a better paying job with health benefits," he finished for her.

"Exactly." Why should she be surprised he knew that, too? Her dossier probably even contained her favorite flavor of Ben & Jerry's ice cream—Cherry Garcia.

"But you regret not being able to make a difference in those people's lives?" he asked.

"Of course."

"This is your chance to change that," he said. "We're making a difference. Our success rate since our inception six months ago is eighty-five percent."

A pretty good stat, but she still didn't see how she fit into their picture. Besides, she'd learned that she did much better calling her own shots. She wasn't an employee of the newspaper; she worked as a freelancer with a steady assignment. She attended a function, wrote it up, and emailed it to her editor.

Cassandra could count on one hand the number of times she'd been in the *Suburban Journal* offices over the last few years. She chafed at the whole office politics thing, another reason she burned out so quickly as a social worker. She wasn't a very social person. "I don't suffer bureaucracy well," she told Demarco.

No grin this time. He laughed. They all laughed. "Neither do we."

"You said you were former FBI," she reminded him.

"With an emphasis on the *former*."

She mulled that one over for a minute. He didn't look like a burned-out type of guy. He looked like he lived for adventure. Maybe the paperwork had gotten to him. Or the office politics. Or having to toe a certain politically correct line. He didn't strike her as a politically correct sort of guy. "You still haven't told me anything more specific about this job."

"I can't. Not until you agree to join us."

Her eyebrows shot toward her hairline as her jaw dropped toward her lap. "Excuse me?" Was the man out of his friggin' mind? "You expect me to accept a position without telling me what that position is? I don't think so. You've told me next to nothing. Where will I be working? What will I be doing? How dangerous is the job?

"I've got kids. They need me. I certainly can't depend on their father if something happens to me." She shook her head back and forth several times. "No, absolutely not. I need more information before I agree to anything."

She then sat back and filled her lungs with air. Her mini-tirade had left her breathless.

Demarco removed a piece of paper from a folder in front of him and sent it sailing down the length of the table toward her. "Will this change your mind?"

She picked up the sheet and turned it over. *Holy-freakin'-moley!* With the salary he had just offered her she'd no longer be at the mercy of The Ex. Hell, she'd be making four times what The Ex made. No worries about whether she'd have enough in the bank to pay the bills each month. No worries about how she'd scrounge up college tuition for her kids. Then there was the benefits package. Fully paid healthcare and an unbelievable pension.

He had her at all those zeroes. She glanced across the table. He knew it, and he knew that she knew he knew it. "When do I start?"

"Now." He rose from his chair, strode down the length of the room to where she sat, and offered her his hand. "Welcome to the team, Cassandra."

Interesting. No more Ms. Davenport. Why did she have the sudden feeling she'd just sold her soul to the devil? Could be that devilish grin plastered across Demarco's face. She reached up and shook his hand. Demarco had one of those perfect handshakes, neither wimpy nor bone crushing forceful. The grin had disappeared. In its place she saw a look of conquest. His eyes told her, "I've got you right where I want you."

Shit! She was so out of her element, she was in another galaxy, but if she were going to Hell, at least she'd have one very sexy tour guide leading the way, and it should prove an interesting trip—if she survived.

Sarcasm was second nature to Cassandra, especially when she was nervous. She'd also been told her sense of humor was an acquired taste. Since Demarco was still holding her hand in his, and she felt an awkward and totally inappropriate tension electrifying the air between the two of them, she resorted to character. "Now do I get the secret decoder ring that answers all my questions?"

Like—what would happen if she changed her mind after she learned the who-what-where-when-and-how of this organization? Would they A) be obliged to kill her, like in *Alias* or B) simply shoot her with an atomizer of forgetfulness, like in *Men in Black*? Neither option appealed to her. So she could only hope she didn't learn anything that would make her change her mind. Or if she did change her mind, that there was an option C.

"They're on back order," he said. "Meanwhile, I'll leave you in the capable hands of Hanna and Noreen. They'll explain everything." He released her hand and exited the room.

FOUR

As it turned out, Cassandra wasn't all that off base when she compared the Mom Squad to a cross between *Alias* and *Men in Black.*

"We like to think of ourselves as one-part *Mission (Semi) Impossible* and one-part *Charlie's (Middle-Aged) Angels,*" said Hanna as they took the hotel elevator to the parking garage.

"Or you could more aptly call us *Big Brother's (Middle-Aged) Angels,*" said Noreen.

"Big brother?"

"We'll explain later." She handed Cassandra a key card. "You'll need this to access the parking garage. Gavin will arrange for one of the techs to install a chip in your car. After today you won't need the key card. The camera will read the chip and automatically open the garage door for you."

Cassandra slipped the plastic into her jacket pocket. "Where are we headed?"

"Morris Ave. in Union," said Hanna. "Just follow us."

Headquarters turned out to be a nondescript three-story red brick office building with a driveway on either side. As Cassandra turned into the driveway, following Hanna and Noreen, she noticed no signage indicating the home of savingtheworld.us— not on the building, nor on any free-standing sign on the postage stamp-sized lawn. Neither did she see written evidence of any other tenants.

Beside the small signs on either side of the building to indicate the one-way nature of the driveway, the building's only other marking was a modest-sized metallic plaque embossed with a street number and mounted to the right of the front entrance.

At the back of the building she followed the directions on the key card machine, dipping the card into the slot and waiting for a green indicator light to blink on before removing it. When the massive metal garage door opened, she drove down a winding ramp to the parking level and pulled into the first vacant space. Hanna and Noreen had already exited their cars and were waiting for her.

The two women led her to a large elevator at the opposite end of the garage. She glanced around, looking for a building directory but found none, neither outside the elevator nor within it. "I see you like to keep a low profile," she said.

"You could say that," said Hanna. She pressed the button on the control panel, and the elevator doors swooshed open.

"I guess we don't take part in Bring Your Kids to Work day?" said Cassandra, stepping inside the elevator.

Noreen laughed as she tapped the button for the second floor. "No kids, no pets."

When the elevator came to a stop, she was led to a room with a small conference table. As the three of them settled into ergonomic black leather upholstered chairs, Cassandra glanced around the room. "You mentioned something earlier about Big Brother. Are we being observed?"

Noreen nodded toward the ceiling. "By the all-seeing cyber-geek on high. Try not to pick your nose."

"No worries. I gave it up for Lent."

Both women laughed. "I think we're going to like working with you," said Hanna.

Noreen nodded.

Cassandra glanced up at the white acoustic ceiling tiles. "I don't see any cameras."

"Trust me, they're everywhere," said Hanna.

Cassandra's mouth dropped open. "Everywhere?"

"Except the ladies' room," said Noreen. "Ever hear of Carnivore?"

She had. "Something to do with Internet surveillance that taps into computers, right?"

Noreen nodded. "Carnivore was developed as an FBI computer program to intercept the communications of suspected criminals, terrorists, and spies."

Cassandra remembered reading a bit about Carnivore in the aftermath of 9/11 as she had fought to find some closure over the loss of her father and brother. She had just started her senior year of high school that day when her world had changed forever.

At first people didn't object to the surveillance. They wanted the government to keep them safe from future attacks. A slight loss of privacy seemed a small price to pay, but the program became a slippery slope that grew increasingly more slippery, leading to Julian Assange and Edward Snowden revealing just how much information the government was collecting on everyone.

"I thought I read somewhere that Carnivore had been terminated," said Cassandra.

"Yes and no," said Noreen. "Carnivore was only one of many spy programs. Others remain. And they're much more sophisticated now."

"There's so much data being collected over cyberspace that the people who are supposed to be protecting us can't keep up," said Hanna. "They have to pick and choose which leads to follow. And because many of today's terrorists are so computer savvy, they often create false trails to misdirect law enforcement."

"Which explains why the bad guys continue to get away with what they do," said Noreen.

"That's where we fit in," said Hanna.

Finally, we were getting down to the nitty-gritty, thought Cassandra. "I'm all ears."

Over the next hour Hanna and Noreen explained the who-what-where-when-and-how to her. "We have eight teams working here," said Hanna. "Four on each of two floors. The basement houses a gym, shower, et cetera. Gavin's apartment, a small cafeteria, and a conference room large enough for all of us to occupy at once are on the third floor."

As a single mother now juggling double duty, Cassandra couldn't help but focus on the more mundane aspects of maintaining such an operation. "Where do you find people you can trust to staff the cafeteria and clean the toilets? Or is that part of the job requirement I've yet to hear?"

Noreen laughed. "Don't worry. We won't be issuing you a toilet brush. We have support staff who have been thoroughly vetted."

For accountability purposes they were known as the Mothers

Advisory Council, MAC for short, an appellation that sounded totally benign for all intents and purposes. Internally they referred to themselves as the Mom Squad, and they were anything but benign if you happened to be on the wrong side of the law.

"MAC is guaranteed not to raise any red flags within the various branches of government should someone start digging," said Noreen. "No congressman is going to waste his time snooping around our business, especially since we never appear as a line item on any budget request."

"Because of the grant from the private sector?"

"Exactly."

"So who is this wealthy benefactor?"

"Liam Hatch," said Hanna.

"I guess you have no budget constraints?" According to *Forbes*, Liam Hatch, a genius computer software developer who preferred to stay out of the spotlight, was reportedly one of the wealthiest men in the country, if not the world.

"None," said Noreen.

From what Cassandra remembered, Hatch also had a vested interest in bringing down terrorists. "He lost some family members to a terrorist attack several years ago, didn't he?"

"His sister and her kids," said Hanna, "in a European train bombing four years ago. They were on vacation."

"Liam and Gavin were college roommates," said Noreen, "The Mom Squad is their brainchild. Liam's sister was Gavin's wife."

A wave of grief washed over Cassandra. She and Demarco—and Hatch—shared a tragic bond.

"So you can see how important this organization is to them," said Hanna.

"And the reason behind their commitment and dedication,"

added Noreen.

"And the government connection?" asked Cassandra, fighting to keep her emotions in check.

"Attorney General Anthony Granville," said Hanna. "The third roommate."

"And someone else who lost a loved one to a terrorist attack," said Cassandra. Granville's aunt had been a passenger on the plane that went down in Shanksville, Pennsylvania on 9/11. What were the odds of three college roommates losing loved ones in terrorist attacks?

However, combining Demarco's expertise, Hatch's unlimited financial resources, and Granville's government connections made for one very unique and powerful organization. And explained how they could operate beneath the government's radar.

"We've all lost someone to terrorism," said Noreen.

Cassandra's mouth dropped open once again. "Are you saying—"

Hanna nodded. "Every member of our organization has a vested interest in taking down terrorists. We've all been directly impacted by terrorism, even the cafeteria and janitorial staff. My husband died in Afghanistan, Noreen's husband in Iraq."

Cassandra jumped to the obvious conclusion. She didn't stumble upon savingtheworld.us; they'd targeted her the moment she began searching for a new job. Big Brother—or more accurately, Liam Hatch—definitely had eyes and ears everywhere, including, apparently, within her computer. The guy had probably created all the software used by the NSA and now employed it— or a version of it—for his own triumvirate-created operation. "You're recruiting people who have a direct connection to terrorism."

Noreen nodded. "Haven't you wished from the moment your father and brother died that you could do something to avenge their deaths?"

Of course she had, but at the time she was only seventeen years old. It wasn't like she could join the army and head off to Afghanistan in search of Osama bin Laden.

"And this is all legal?" she asked once more, even though Demarco had already assured her it was. The idea of a quasi-government agency that most of the government knew nothing about raised more than a few red flags for her, and once again Cassandra began to question her own sanity in accepting a job offer that didn't outline her specific duties and responsibilities ahead of time.

"Perfectly legal and legitimate," said Hanna. "Like Gavin said, those who need to know are well-aware of us. We're the secret weapons in the fight against crime."

Which puts an all-new spin on the term Supermom.

"We do mostly computer surveillance," continued Hanna, "although there are times we're out in the field. As we already mentioned, middle-aged moms blend into the woodwork and can snoop around and eavesdrop without drawing suspicion to themselves. No one pays any attention to us."

So true. How often had she been ignored by store clerks or worse yet, bypassed for the younger, cuter customer standing next to her? When was the last time she had walked past a construction site and heard a wolf whistle? Not that she'd ever appreciated them, but none had been directed toward her in more than a decade.

Noreen continued to explain the savingtheworld.us

organizational chart. "Gavin reports directly to Carla Jordan who oversees a half dozen MAC satellite groups across the country. When we identify a possible threat, Carla coordinates with Granville to determine the best course of action and which agencies to call in, depending on the situation."

"I've heard that name before," said Cassandra. "Didn't the government accuse her of treason?"

"Don't believe everything you read in the newspapers," said Noreen. "Carla is one of the good guys. She's saved more lives than you can imagine."

"Then why—?"

"Politics," said Hanna, practically spitting out the word.

"I see." Although she wasn't sure she did, but she pushed that thought to the back of her brain for now. "And you've been so successful that you're expanding the operation?" asked Cassandra.

Noreen and Hanna exchanged a quick glance before Hanna answered. "In a manner of speaking. We've found that we work best in teams of three. This is the Greek Satellite. We're Alpha Team. Gavin's other teams are Beta, Gamma, Delta, Epsilon, Theta, Sigma, and Omega. The teams in the other satellites have their own unique designations. One chose planets, for instance, another mountain ranges."

"There are only two of you," said Cassandra. "Am I replacing someone?" She caught Hanna dart another quick glance toward Noreen as some silent communication passed between them.

"That's right," said Noreen.

"Why did she leave?"

"She didn't quite work out," said Hanna. "Not everyone does."

The stern set of Hanna's mouth told Cassandra she wouldn't be hearing any further details regarding her predecessor. Another red flag sprang up in her gray matter.

"For the next couple of months you'll spend part of your day going through training sessions," said Noreen. "But at the same time you'll be working alongside us, learning as you work."

"What kind of training?" she asked.

"Everything from various computer software programs to self-defense."

"Self-defense?" The red flags were now sprouting up in every nook and cranny of her brain.

"Every woman should know basic self-defense," said Hanna. "You may never have the need to use it, but it's still a skill worth acquiring."

Cassandra supposed that made sense, whether she was a member of the Mom Squad or not, especially as a single woman. Muggers lurked everywhere, even in upscale New Jersey suburbs, and she'd been putting off taking a self-defense course for too long. Just like she'd put off any form of exercise, no matter how much she needed it. Maybe a side benefit of this job would be losing that muffin top and underarm jiggle.

She eyed her fellow Moms. Neither one of them had the figure of a Victoria's Secret model, but neither did they have muffin tops nor sagging upper arm flesh from what she could see. They both looked like they could run a marathon; she'd have trouble finishing a fifty-yard dash.

While Cassandra wrapped her mind around the idea of breaking bricks with a hand chop and disabling a three hundred pound thug with a well-placed elbow jab to the solar plexus, Hanna continued speaking, "We'll give you a quick tour, grab some lunch, then process you."

"Process?"

"All the requisite paperwork and then some," said Noreen. "Rules and regs. Gotta follow them even if we're off the government radar."

~*~

Four hours later Cassandra arrived home, having been fingerprinted, photographed, and processed in triplicate to the nth power. She'd received a state-of-the-art smart phone with enough bells and whistles to make her iPhone look like a Fisher-Price toddler toy. She was instructed to keep it charged and with her at all times. She'd also received a cover story about her new job. No one was to know who she really worked for or what she really did.

"We'd have to kill you and anyone you blabbed to," said Hanna.

Cassandra had looked from her to Noreen, then back to Hanna. Both had worn deadly serious expressions—emphasis on the *deadly*. But then Hanna had grinned. "Only kidding about the killing part," she said.

"But seriously," Noreen had added. "What we do is never to go beyond us and Gavin. We don't even discuss our work with other Mom Squad teams unless it's an operation that requires a larger task force. We can't afford to jeopardize a mission."

Cassandra had nodded that she understood, but she wasn't a hundred percent sure they were only kidding about the killing part. As she prepared dinner, she once again pondered what the hell she'd gotten herself into.

I guess I'll find out soon enough.

~*~

Later that evening as she ate dinner with her kids, Cassandra told her first lie about her new job.

"What exactly does the Mothers Advisory Council do?" asked twelve-year-old Hayley, talking around a mouthful of lasagna.

"We study current and proposed legislation that impacts families, then we make recommendations regarding changes." The lie slipped out of her mouth with an ease that startled her. Meet Cassandra Davenport, Mata Hari Mom.

"Sounds boring," said Hayley's twin brother Cooper.

"It pays well and comes with benefits," said Cassandra. "I can do boring." But something told her that her life would never again be boring.

"Whatever." Cooper shoveled a huge forkful of the lasagna into his mouth.

The twins were at that age where kids often spoke to their parents mostly in monosyllables—if they spoke to them at all. She knew part of Cooper's belligerent attitude was due to the divorce and his father's abdication of parental responsibility, not that The Ex had ever embraced parenthood when they were married.

The other part she chalked up to the beginnings of the hormonal rollercoaster that hit all adolescents. Cassandra knew she was only at the beginning of what would be a long and tumultuous ride. If she lived long enough, she might survive to see her kids come out the other side of the hormonal maelstrom.

The Ex's recent marriage to the Double-D had only compounded Cooper's insolence. Like all children of divorce, he and his sister had harbored a secret hope that their parents would eventually reunite. The impending birth of what her kids viewed as replacement twins killed that hope.

When they were married, she and The Ex had discussed eventually having kids at some point in the future. So she'd been completely blindsided by his fury over the failed birth control that had resulted in the conception of Cooper and Haley. Ironically, The Ex seemed more than happy to marry Double-D when confronted by her pregnancy.

"How much are you going to be making?" asked Cooper, drawing her back into the here and now.

"None of your business."

"Mo-om!"

"Enough that we don't have to worry about losing the house if your father continues down his Deadbeat Dad path."

"Enough for me to get a car for my sixteenth birthday?"

She stared at the hopeful expression on her son's face. Maybe a breadcrumb would go a long way toward an attitude adjustment. Besides, she had four years to worry about it. "Possibly."

Mr. Belligerent morphed into Mr. Happy Face, his dark brown eyes growing wide, a smile spreading from ear to ear. "Really?"

"I said 'possibly.' We'll see how things pan out—including keeping your grades up."

"Cool! I can't wait to tell the guys." With that he jumped out of his chair and headed upstairs without so much as a may-I-be-excused? Or clearing his plate.

"I guess he didn't hear the 'possibly,'" said Hayley.

"Parenting Lesson Number One," said Cassandra. "Kids only hear what they want to hear. Remember that."

"I hear you, Mom."

"Right. I'll remind you of that the next time you ignore me."

In typical Hayley fashion she stuck out her tongue. Cassandra stuck hers back at her daughter. Then they both shared a laugh. She wished she could freeze the moment because she certainly knew Hayley hadn't escaped the attack of the raging hormones. She knew it was only a matter of time.

FIVE

The next morning Cassandra dressed in a black A-line skirt, black fitted T-shirt, and black blazer for her first full day as the newest member of the Mom Squad. She assumed black was the official uniform, even though no one had mentioned an office dress code. Fine by her. She had plenty of black in her wardrobe, given its slimming properties.

When she drove down the driveway to the garage entrance, the door magically rose in front of her. She parked her car and took the elevator to the second floor, arriving ten minutes early. Noreen and Hanna must have been monitoring the security cameras because they greeted her as she stepped from the elevator. Either that or Big Brother had alerted them to her arrival.

The thought of constant surveillance unnerved her. No, she didn't pick her nose, but would the high-tech spying software record how often she scratched an itch or took a pee break? Did it monitor her caloric intake at lunch? Send down a laser beam to shock her if her eyelids grew heavy mid-afternoon? Or notify someone in the cafeteria to bring her a cup of coffee?

She had no chance to ask any of these pressing questions, though, because within minutes she found herself huddled in front of an enormous computer monitor with Noreen and Hanna seated on either side of her. Her two other team members explained how they sifted through the hundreds of thousands of pieces of data scoured by Liam Hatch's software.

"It's like a huge jigsaw puzzle," explained Hanna. "Liam has designed specific programs to look for certain patterns and keywords, and the programs are always being refined and tweaked. But even the most sophisticated software can only go so far before the human element is required."

"Much of what we do involves gut instinct," added Noreen. "Finding pieces that fit together where the program found no correlations or dots to connect because the dots were so far apart and hidden within other information."

They showed her a few examples of previous cases, including evidence they'd uncovered that led to the arrest of a Chinese arms dealer and the group of white supremacists he'd supplied with nearly a hundred Russian Kalashnikov rifles.

"One part gut instinct, one part mind reading," said Cassandra as she read through the documentation.

"Yeah, the alphabets didn't pick up on those guys at all," said Noreen. "If it wasn't for something Hanna noticed, the True Believers, as they called themselves, would have succeeded in their plan to mow down countless Green Bay Packers fans in the stadium parking lot as they headed back to their cars after a game."

"They earned their salaries that week," said Demarco, coming up behind them. He passed file folders to the two other women. "Take a look at these." Then he turned to Cassandra. "You're with me."

She reached for her purse.

"You won't need that," he said. "We're not leaving the building."

She hesitated for a split second before the absurdity of her second-nature action hit her. This place was as secure as Fort Knox, if not more so. She could leave the Crown Jewels sitting on her desk with full confidence they'd still be there when she returned.

Demarco led her to the elevator and once inside hit the button for the basement. When the doors opened, she found herself in a narrow concrete hallway. Demarco headed for the first door on the left and punched a code into the panel on the wall. The door sprung open to reveal the "et cetera" Hanna had referred to the day before—a firing range.

Cassandra spun around to confront him. "I told you I don't do guns. You agreed."

"I said we'd discuss it."

"This doesn't look like a discussion to me."

"You need to learn how to protect yourself."

"From sitting at a computer terminal all day?"

He removed a gun and a clip from a locked cabinet. "This is a Glock," he said, fitting the clip into the gun. "You won't always be sitting at a computer terminal. There will be times when you're out in the field. I need to know that you'll be prepared for whatever might go down. That you're capable of taking care of yourself and watching your team's back. They'll be doing the same for you."

He grabbed her elbow and led her over to one of three counters. "Put these on." He handed her safety glasses and a neon green plastic hearing protection earmuff that hung from a hook on the wall.

She glanced from him to the glasses and earmuff to the gun and back to him. "I suppose it's not a smart idea to argue with a guy holding a gun."

"You catch on quickly."

"I don't suppose there's a human resources person I can file a complaint with over this."

"You're looking at him."

"Swell." She placed the glasses on her face and the hearing protection over her ears. Demarco turned her to face the target at the far end of an enclosed tunnel that stretched beyond the counter. He came up behind her and grabbed both of her hands, positioning them around the gun. "Spread your legs," he said.

She moved her feet to either side a few inches.

"More." He inserted a leg between both of hers and spread her feet wider. Then he raised her arms. "Lock your elbows."

She locked her elbows.

He drew her into his chest—his extremely hard chest. Gavin Demarco was all six-pack abs and not an inch of flab. She glanced at his exposed forearms. All taut muscle and sinew. All business.

"Now sight the target and pull the trigger." He gently squeezed his finger over hers. The room erupted in a thunderous explosion, the recoil slamming her deeper into his chest—and lower, equally hard, parts of his body. She quickly shifted her weight forward as he dropped his arms.

When her heart stopped knocking against her own chest, she looked down the tunnel at the target, a silhouette of a figure. A hole pierced the poor guy's head.

Demarco stepped away from her. "Try it by yourself."

A cool breeze kissed her back in place of the searing heat of his body. She wanted the heat back. It had been too long since a man had held her. Now all she felt was empty.

"Ready?" he asked.

"As ready as I'll ever be," she answered, wondering if he detected the tremor in her voice. She stood the way he'd shown her, raised her arms, locked her elbows, and fired.

"Now try it with your eyes open, Cassandra."

She looked down the tunnel. Wherever her bullet had landed, it hadn't hit anywhere near the target.

He had her practice for half an hour. By the time they'd finished she felt like she'd been subjected to a form of Medieval rack torture. The tension within her had taken refuge in her less-than-toned muscles, and they weren't shy about protesting against the intrusion. But she'd started hitting the target nearly seventy-five percent of the time.

An unexpected sense of accomplishment swept through her. Back in junior and senior high, her lack of athletic ability meant she was always chosen last for any mandatory team sport. She'd never mastered the fine art of landing any ball anywhere remotely near its designated spot—whether softball, volleyball, or tennis ball.

She still hated guns, but after only half an hour she was batting .750, mixed-metaphorically speaking. She'd never come close to a stat like that in any gym activity. However, Gavin Demarco better not expect her to climb a rope because she really sucked at that. Factor in the added underarm jiggle developed over the last two decades, and she knew the only .750 stat would be the percentage of an inch she *might* be able to raise herself. However, even that was doubtful.

"You'll practice half an hour a day, every day for the next few months," said Gavin. "I want you hitting the kill zone every time."

What! .750 *wasn't good enough for him?* Her body told him to go to hell, but her mouth stayed firmly shut. If she protested, he'd probably make her practice an hour a day.

~*~

Cassandra spent the remainder of the morning absorbing additional computer instruction from Noreen and Hanna. At twelve-thirty the three women broke for lunch and headed up to the cafeteria where Cassandra was introduced to some of the members of the other Greek teams and various support personnel. However, after filling their trays, Hanna led them to an empty table rather than choosing to sit with anyone else.

"No fraternizing among the troops?" asked Cassandra as she settled into her seat.

"Not unless we're working together on an investigation," said Noreen.

"And even then," added Hanna, "Gavin has a strict policy about not discussing cases outside of our own areas unless he's authorized it. We don't even talk shop among our own team members here."

"Why?"

"To prevent contamination," said Noreen.

Something else she didn't understand but decided not to question at this time. To her way of thinking, more ears and eyes on a case could only help, but Gavin apparently had his reasons. If Noreen and Hanna knew what they were, neither was offering her any further explanation at this time.

~*~

For the remainder of the day Cassandra alternated between

mental and physical training. The mental training consisted of learning to use various computer programs and studying previous cases. The physical training involved a masochist named Hawkeye Barnstable, ex-marine and official savingtheworld.us personal trainer.

After changing into workout clothes waiting for her in the locker room, Cassandra entered the gym at her designated time. The first thing she did was scan the ceiling for evidence of climbing ropes. Finding none, she breathed a sigh of relief.

The massive gym with its polished wooden floor contained one of every piece of exercise equipment she'd ever seen advertised on TV, along with half a dozen machines completely foreign to her. They were spaced out in two rows running the length of one wall. Gymnastics equipment lined the wall opposite the workout machines. Another area was devoted to weights and a bench press. Several sparring bags hung from the ceiling. Floor mats hung from pegs along all four walls except for the small glass-enclosed office located in a corner to the right of the entrance.

Unfortunately, Cassandra's initial relief over not finding any climbing ropes was short-lived. After two hours of high-intensity workouts and martial arts disciplines—most of which she'd never heard of nor could properly pronounce—every cell of her body screamed *uncle!* Thankfully, two hours into the torture session the trainer finally gave her a reprieve. "That's enough for today, Davenport."

Bent at the waist, hands on her knees, and dripping sweat, Cassandra desperately tried to pull oxygen into her lungs. "How'd...I...do?"

The masochist barked out a laugh. "For someone who hasn't exercised in nearly twenty years, if ever? You tell me."

She tilted her chin up to glance at him. "That good, huh?" The guy made her feel like a wuss. According to Noreen, he'd lost a leg during the Boston Marathon bombing, yet he went on to run in the race the following year—and won!

"Hit the showers, Davenport. Then soak in the whirlpool for fifteen minutes."

She would have saluted him if only she could raise her arm high enough.

And I thought target practice hurt like hell!

~*~

By the time five o'clock arrived, she could barely move. An hour in the whirlpool wouldn't have been nearly enough time to soothe her aching muscles. She couldn't remember how many muscles there were in the human body, but she was certain every single one of them now screamed out in protest against the torture they'd endured today.

Sitting in front of a computer screen after her stint in the gym only served to compound the problem, turning her as stiff as the Tin Woodsman—before Dorothy oiled him. She stifled a wince when she rose from her chair, but apparently, she hadn't done as well at masking the expression on her face.

"Epsom salts," said Noreen. "Soak for at least an hour before you go to bed tonight."

"It gets easier," added Hanna. She reached into a desk drawer, withdrew a single dosage pack of Motrin, and handed it to Cassandra. "This will help."

"Thanks." Damn! It even hurt to speak. She must have been clenching her jaw against the pain without realizing it.

She tore open the packet and downed the two caplets, washing the pills down with a swig from her water bottle. "How long before it starts getting easier?"

Hanna shrugged. "A week or two."

"Or three," said Noreen.

She focused from one to the other. Neither looked anything but serious. This time Cassandra didn't bother masking a moan. "Three weeks!"

"Depends," said Noreen. "No two bodies respond the same to a new exercise regimen."

New? That assumed she had a previous exercise regimen. Apparently, walking up and down supermarket aisles and lugging baskets of laundry up and down two flights of stairs didn't count.

"Assuming I survive that long." Which she seriously doubted. Right now, she wasn't sure she could walk to the elevator, let alone get in her car and drive home.

"Epsom salts," repeated Noreen. "And a good night's sleep. You'll feel better in the morning."

"Three weeks," she muttered as she shuffled down the hall to the elevator. "I'll never make it."

Behind her, she thought she heard a deep masculine laugh, but when she turned around, no one was there.

SIX

Masking her pain and exhaustion from her kids that night seriously tested her thespian skills. They became suspicious the moment she walked into the house with cartons of Chinese take-out. After their initial delight at the midweek treat, they continued to eye her with concern when they thought she didn't notice. She noticed.

Finally, Hayley said, "You okay, Mom?"

She forced a smile. "Of course."

"You don't look so good," said Cooper.

"What do you mean?"

"You look like you're in pain," he said. "You weren't in an accident, were you?"

"No, of course not. I'm just tired. I'm not used to working full-time in an office."

"You wouldn't lie to us, would you?" asked Hayley.

"I was not in an accident. Go check the car if you don't believe me. You won't find a dent or a scratch."

Cooper knit his brows together. "You weren't hit be a car while crossing the street, were you?"

Cassandra placed her chopsticks on her plate. "Would you like to check me for scrapes and bruises?"

The twins glanced at each other before shaking their heads. "I'll pass," said Cooper.

She raised an eyebrow at her daughter. "Hayley?"

"If you say you're not sick or hurt," I believe you."

"I'm not sick or hurt."

"Okay, but I don't understand how you can look the way you do after a day of sitting at a desk, reading papers."

Cassandra sighed. Her kids might be at the age where they were becoming extremely self-centered, but that didn't negate that they were also smart and observant. She'd have to come up with better ways to dance around the truth.

"I haven't worked full-time in an office since before giving birth to both of you. New jobs are stressful. There's much more involved than simply doing the job you were assigned."

"Like what?" asked Cooper.

"It's like being dropped into the middle of a new school where everyone else already knows each other really well. Being the new kid on the block is hard work. You have to prove yourself."

"How long does that take?" asked Hayley.

"Hopefully, no more than three weeks."

"Cool! Three weeks of take-out," said Cooper.

Cassandra picked up her chopsticks, "See? There's an upside to everything."

~*~

Two weeks into her training, Cassandra had mastered the various technical aspects of her new job. She still hated her half-hour each day at the firing range, primarily because she hated guns. And always would. Her feelings had not gotten in the way of improving her marksmanship, though.

Just call me Annie Oakley.

However, she hoped she'd never have to use the Glock outside of the basement firing range. Shooting at a paper target was one thing but a flesh and blood human being? She didn't know how law enforcement and military personnel managed to stay sane after taking the life of another person, even under kill-or-be-killed situations. Maybe they didn't. Maybe that's why so many developed PTSD.

She still dreaded her two-hour workouts in the gym each day, but her muscles had begun to adapt to the vigorous pace Hawkeye forced on her. It helped that she noticed her muffin top was disappearing, and her underarms had less jiggle to them. Who knew exercise actually worked?

She returned from her latest torture session to find Gavin deep in discussion with Noreen and Hanna. All three paused as she entered the room, the two women darting a quick look in her direction before focusing their attention back on Gavin.

After nodding toward her, Gavin addressed Noreen and Hanna, "We'll discuss this further at a later time."

Another red flag announced itself. What was up? On the surface they appeared to trust her, but Cassandra sensed a definite undercurrent of something else going on, something Gavin and her two teammates were keeping to themselves.

Part of her understood that two weeks wasn't nearly enough time to gain the trust of her coworkers, not with the type of work they did. However, they had vetted her sufficiently to know they could trust her. It annoyed her that there were obviously things they felt necessary to keep from her at this point. Perhaps that would eventually change.

Or maybe whatever was going on was above her pay grade. There was a hierarchy at savingtheworld.us, like any other corporation. If she needed to know something, she assumed they'd tell her. For now, she knew better than to pry—no matter how much their actions piqued her curiosity.

~*~

After Cassandra left for the day, Gavin invited Noreen and Hanna to join him in his apartment. He poured them each a glass of Merlot and grabbed a bottle of Sam Adams for himself before joining them around the kitchen island. "What's your assessment of our newest recruit? Think she'll work out?"

"She's still pissed as hell over the guns," said Noreen.

"Tell me something I don't know," he said. If the woman had been able to spit nails, his hide would now be tacked up to the wall of the firing range. Although, he wasn't sure whether her fury stemmed from his deceit or the boner that had surprised the hell out of him—and her— on that first day, given the expression she'd fought hard to mask. Probably equal parts of both.

He'd keep that information to himself, though. He might expect his teams to share everything with him, but information didn't necessarily flow all the time in both directions—at least not that sort of information.

Why Cassandra Davenport? He'd never reacted in that way to any of the other women he'd trained, and plenty of them had slammed into his body the first time they experienced a gun's recoil. In hindsight he realized part of him hadn't wanted to let go of her afterwards. Her soft curves had fit so perfectly against him.

Gavin shook the thought from his mind. He had no time for

such things. What mattered was that Cassandra hadn't walked out. Pissed or not, she'd continued to shoot, and he'd been impressed with how quickly her aim improved. Anger and accuracy generally don't mix well.

Gavin chuckled. "Pissed or not, she's a crackerjack shot. And after only two weeks of practice. Hard to believe she'd never held a gun before."

"Do we know she hasn't?" asked Noreen. "Maybe there's a reason she hates guns."

"You mean like being robbed at gunpoint or witnessing a shooting?" asked Hanna.

Noreen shrugged. "Just saying."

"Nothing came up in our investigation of her," said Gavin.

"Not all crimes are reported," said Noreen.

"True."

"Maybe we should ask her," said Hanna. "If there's something in her background that we don't know—"

"Do it," said Gavin. "We need to know we can count on her no matter what."

"When do we read her in on this new intel?" asked Noreen. "Assuming you don't want to keep it from her at this point."

Gavin downed his beer, then huffed out his frustration. He'd wanted Cassandra fully trained before exposing her to any out-of-office ops. He didn't need another member of his team going rogue, as was the case with her predecessor. He'd learned a hard lesson that day and had no desire to repeat his mistake with Cassandra. However, a recent threat uncovered by Delta Team made that a luxury he could no longer afford.

Normally each team operated independently from the others, but none of his teams had ever uncovered a plot that involved a relative of another team member. Until now.

He thought about the Boston police captain who had discovered that his own son planned to blow up a college cafeteria and carry out beheadings in the name of ISIS. When the father first sensed something was out of whack with his son, the kid wasn't even a blip on any government agency surveillance. Luckily, the father didn't ignore his own gut instincts. He called the FBI and averted a catastrophic attack.

It takes a certain type of man to be able to come to terms with the horrific revelation that his own flesh and blood is a monster—let alone have the courage to turn him in to the authorities.

Cassandra was smart enough to figure out Gavin had targeted her for one of his teams. He hadn't expected anything less based on what he'd learned about her. What she didn't know was why.

He knew she harbored no love for her ex-husband, but nothing Gavin or his staff had unearthed led them to believe Cassandra had the slightest inkling of Michael Schuster's darker side. Her ex apparently kept his inner monster confined within the anonymity of the Internet.

When noise about the guy first began to surface, MAC didn't pay too much attention to him. Schuster appeared to be, like so many others, nothing more than a loudmouthed reactionary malcontent. Gavin's teams came across hundreds of guys like Schuster on a daily basis. Most never advanced beyond shooting off their mouths on social media and ranting on blogs few people ever read. Most. Not all.

Delta Team dug around but found no connection between the middle-aged pharmaceutical salesman and any known terrorists. Still, they continued to monitor him and those like him. They knew yesterday's run-of-the-mill loudmouthed malcontent could morph into tomorrow's mass murderer. Terrorist organizations had a way of zeroing in on people like Michael Schuster and radicalizing them.

Gavin had recruited Cassandra on the off chance that Michael Schuster might eventually move from all-talk to plotting deadly action. And now he had.

When Schuster recently began purchasing bleach, drain cleaner, and acetone in quantities far greater than anyone would need for washing clothes, unclogging pipes, and removing nail polish, Gavin suspected one of the terrorist organizations had scored itself another member. Without a doubt, Michael Schuster was stockpiling bomb-making materials.

What Gavin needed to find out was when and where he planned to set off his bomb and who else was involved. That's where Cassandra came in. As his ex-wife she'd be able to snoop around without raising suspicion. Aside from one mistake, once again, his instincts had been correct in his choice of recruits.

"I'll take the lead on reading Cassandra in on the situation," he told Noreen and Hanna. "I want the two of you to coordinate with Delta Team. We need as much information as quickly as possible in order to prevent whatever this guy is planning."

~*~

The next morning Cassandra was scheduled to meet with Hawkeye at eight o'clock. After changing into her workout clothes, she entered the gym, stopped short, and froze.

"Something wrong?" asked Hawkeye.

She pointed to the rope he stood next to. "That wasn't here before."

"So? It's here now."

"You don't expect me to climb that, do you?"

"Why? You scared of heights?"

"No, I'm fine with heights."

"Then what's the problem?"

"I failed rope climbing every single year in school. Junior and senior high. I can't do it."

"Sure, you can."

She shook her head. "No, I can't."

Hawkeye offered her a sadistic grin. "Wanna bet?"

"How about if I do twice as many pushups today?"

"How about if you get your ass over here and climb this rope, Davenport?"

"I'm telling you I can't."

"And I'm telling you we're going to stay here until you do. I've been tasked with whipping you into shape by Gavin's deadline, and I never blow off a deadline."

"Which is?"

He offered her another sadistic grin. "Trust me. You don't want to know."

Two hours later, Cassandra was covered in rope burns, and her arms were on fire, but she'd finally made it to the top of the rope.

"Told you so," said Hawkeye.

She stared down at him. "Can I come down now?"

He pulled a watch from his pocket and tapped the screen. "In ten minutes."

"What? Are you freaking crazy? I can't hold on for ten minutes!"

"If you come down sooner, you climb up again."

"This is abuse!"

"Take it up with management." He turned and headed toward his glass-walled office where he settled into a leather chair while he kept an eye on her.

Cassandra closed her eyes and held on for dear life.

Ten minutes later Hawkeye stepped from his office and yelled to her. "Times up, Davenport. Climb down and hit the showers. Meet me at the practice range at twelve-hundred hours."

She collapsed flat on her back onto the mat. "That's noon, right?"

He grunted as he headed back to his office.

Cassandra had been under the impression that Gavin would continue training her in the use of firearms, but after the first day he'd turned her over to Hawkeye.

She wondered if the change in instructor had to do with a certain piece of Gavin's equipment that had sprung to attention when the Glock's recoil sent her hurling against his torso.

As shocked as she'd been, a part of her had wanted to respond. Years had passed since she'd had a particular itch scratched by someone rather than something, and she was surprised to realize she wouldn't mind Gavin Demarco relieving that itch.

Bad idea. Any relationship beyond a purely professional one was a disaster waiting to happen.

Besides, saluting anatomy or not, Demarco was all business. Nothing would ever happen between them. Assigning Hawkeye to take over for him made that clear. Maybe someday she'd meet someone who would replace her motorized companion, but that someone wouldn't be Gavin Demarco.

"I'll take that as a yes," she called to Hawkeye's departing back. The guy had the physique of a fireplug and the face of a pug. She'd had no problem keeping her mind focused with him instructing her—when she wasn't focused on the aches and pains he caused her.

Cassandra hoisted herself to her feet and glanced up at the wall-mounted clock as she crossed the gym to the locker room. Ninety short minutes before she subjected her body to more grueling pain—assuming she'd be able to drag herself out of the whirlpool once she settled into it. The odds weren't looking all that great right now.

She stripped off the sweat-soaked workout clothes, dropped them in the laundry hamper, and stepped into one of the three shower stalls. Once she scrubbed the sweat and dirt off her body and washed her hair, she settled into the whirlpool and closed her eyes.

All she needed now was a frothy cocktail with a maraschino cherry, a wedge of pineapple, and a paper umbrella. Maybe then she could forget about her bruised flesh and aching muscles. Too bad she lacked the strength to raise a glass to her lips. Not that the locker room included a wet bar. The Three Musketeers had definitely dropped the ball when it came to designing this particular section of the MAC facility.

Five minutes into her soak the locker room door banged open and she heard Gavin yell, "Cassandra, my office in five."

"Is that a literal five-minutes?" she asked.

The door slammed shut without a response. So much for her fifteen-minute reprieve! She wondered if she'd be able to add the ten minutes owed her to tomorrow's whirlpool session. And how the hell was she supposed to dry her hair in less than five minutes? No way that was happening if she wanted to come anywhere close to meeting his deadline.

She reluctantly hoisted herself out of the whirlpool, quickly dried off, dressed, and combed her wet hair into a ponytail. Somehow she managed to knock on Gavin's office door within the allotted timeframe.

"Come in." She stepped into the room and found Gavin engrossed in something on his computer screen. Tension filled his features. Without looking up, he waved his hand, motioning her to the seating area at the opposite end of the room where she found a small sofa, weathered wood coffee table, and two side chairs. "Close the door and have a seat."

Cassandra opted for the gray microfiber sofa because the matching chairs were positioned with their backs facing his desk. "Is something wrong?" she asked, noticing that his scowl had deepened even further.

Had she already screwed up? She'd done everything she'd been asked to do, and short of him blindsiding her with the Glock and target practice on the first day, she'd done so without complaint.

Well, almost without complaint. She'd certainly made her feelings known to Hawkeye in the gym today. Chances were, he'd reported to Gavin while she hung for dear life twelve feet above the floor. Or for all she knew, Gavin had observed her entire torture session from the comfort of his leather office chair.

However, in the end, she'd made it to the top of the rope and had held on for the allotted ten minutes. That had to count for something. Three hours ago, even if someone had held a gun to her head, she doubted she'd have been able to haul herself twelve inches off the floor, let alone twelve feet.

But maybe this had more to do with hormones. Even though neither of them had given voice to what had occurred two weeks ago, it had to be on his mind as much as it was on hers. Given his grim expression, Cassandra concluded Gavin was canning her to keep her from becoming a distraction.

Did this constitute a reverse form of sexual discrimination?

How do you file a complaint with the government when, as far as the government is concerned, your place of employment doesn't exist?

"Something is definitely wrong," he said.

Cassandra braced herself. Maybe he'd at least offer her a decent severance package, but what was the likelihood of that after only two weeks of employment? And forget about any letter of recommendation, given they officially didn't exist.

Gavin tore his attention away from his computer screen and rose from his desk. He crossed the room and took a seat in the chair closest to her. His expression hadn't changed, but now that he sat inches away from her, she noticed what she had first read as anger was something else. She suddenly realized that Gavin Demarco's tension most likely stemmed from carrying the weight of the world on his shoulders. Something on that computer screen had scared the hell out of him.

He stared directly into her eyes. "We need to have a talk about something I was hoping to put off at least until you were fully trained, if not forever."

She heaved a silent sigh of relief and sent up a quick prayer to whichever saint looks out for single moms trying to stay afloat. That statement certainly didn't sound like the preamble to a dismissal. "About what?"

"Your ex-husband."

Cassandra stared dumbfounded. Of all the subjects Gavin might raise, The Ex was the last topic she'd expect him to choose. After all, she and Michael had been divorced for five years. His wandering hormones and penchant for Double-D's just shy of jailbait were now the current Double-D's problem. Other than when he remembered to exercise his visitation rights, her contact with him remained minimal and more often than not, occurred either in judge's chambers or a courtroom.

When she found her voice, she said, "With all the resources at your disposal, you probably know more about him at this point than I do."

"You need to know what I know, and I need your help in stopping him."

If the subject of Michael had caught her by surprise, this last comment totally blindsided her. She studied the man sitting across from her. She had wondered why, of all the people he could recruit for MAC, he had zeroed in on her. She had no skills that made her a candidate for a counterterrorism organization. Yet here she was, and there could be only one reason that set her apart from all the other candidates—assuming there even were other candidates, which at this moment she seriously doubted.

Gavin had just confirmed her suspicions with a doozy of a revelation. "You recruited me for a specific purpose, didn't you? That entire job interview was a total sham."

He nodded. "Staged."

"Because of Michael?

Gavin nodded again. "We needed to create a scenario where we'd be able to trust you to keep our secrets."

"You could have just told me the truth."

"We couldn't run the risk of you not cooperating. Or worse yet, reporting us to the authorities or the media. One phone call and our entire operation could be compromised."

Now that she knew as much as she did about savingtheworld.us—or MAC—she understood the deception. "You can't possibly think Michael's mixed up in some terrorist plot." Michael Schuster possessed many less-than-admirable qualities. Deadbeat dad and cheating scumbag topped the list—but terrorist? Absurd! Except Gavin's expression said otherwise.

"Delta Team has had an eye on Schuster for some time."

"Why?"

"Are you aware of his social media presence?"

"I didn't know he had one. My contact with him is extremely limited."

"He's been ranting on social media platforms for months. That's not necessarily uncommon, but sometimes it's a precursor to criminal activity."

She braced herself for the worst. "What have you discovered?"

"We have reason to believe he's stockpiling materials to build a bomb. Either one extremely large bomb or multiple smaller ones."

"There must be some mistake."

"I'm afraid not."

Cassandra leaned her head back on the sofa and closed her eyes. How could she have lived with a man for so many years and not realized the evil he harbored within him? She opened her eyes, leaned forward, and sighed. "Tell me what the bastard's done."

"As I'm sure you've already learned, one of the things we monitor for is larger than normal purchases of certain common household materials that could be used in bomb-making."

She nodded. "Like lawn fertilizer or pressure cookers."

"As well as bleach, drain cleaner, and acetone, the components for making TATP."

"What's that?"

"The type of bomb used by the shoe and underwear bombers. It's also known as Mother of Satan. It's unbelievably simple to make, but the results can be quite disastrous."

"And Michael has purchased these items in large quantities?"

"I'm guessing he thought he wouldn't raise any suspicions by paying cash for them."

"You were able to track his transactions without him using his credit cards?"

"Delta Team discovered he purchased the chemicals from various wholesale clubs, driving to locations throughout the tri-state area over the course of the last week, often hitting several stores within a few hours. What he didn't realize was that because of his memberships, a digitized record is kept of his purchases, even when he pays cash for items."

Michael never thought through the ramifications of his actions. However, his past actions had only resulted in the death of his marriage, not the possible slaughter of hundreds of people. Or more. "Delta Team monitored his membership accounts?"

"Over the last few weeks his social media postings had grown more incendiary. I had Delta Team dig deeper, and they came up with the chemical purchases."

"If you suspect he's building a bomb, why not bring in bomb-sniffing dogs or some other form of detection equipment? Couldn't you check around the perimeter of his house when he's at work to verify your suspicions, then obtain a search warrant?"

"It's not that simple. One of the problems with TATP is that it's extremely difficult to detect through normal means."

"*One* of the problems? There are others?"

"The bombs are highly unstable and hazardous to defuse. For this reason TATP is now the bomb of choice for terrorists. The materials are readily available in hardware stores, big box stores, and even supermarkets, as well as online. To make matters worse, with a few keystrokes any would-be terrorist can find instructions for assembling such a bomb on the Internet."

Cassandra now understood the source of the frown lines that covered Gavin's face. This was the sort of thing he dealt with on a daily basis. And what probably kept him up at night.

The reality of the world she'd entered had just become much more than real to her. Stopping anonymous terrorists before they struck was one thing, but learning a suspected terrorist was her own ex-husband? That made everything a lot more personal.

Still, she found it hard to wrap her head around Michael going that far off the deep end. "There are no legitimate reasons for having all of these items?"

"In the quantities Schuster has acquired? None."

She shook her head. "This is too bizarre to believe. When would he have become radicalized? In all the years we were married he never espoused any anti-American rhetoric other than at tax time each year." And who hasn't grumbled and cursed the government every April while preparing their tax returns?

She rose from the couch, walked over to the window, and gazed down on the street at the dozens of people driving past the nondescript MAC building, never suspecting she and the others inside might be the only people standing between them and a terrorist's bomb. How many of those suburban moms out running errands in their SUVs and minivans might one day die at the hands of some twisted homegrown terrorist?

Or were some of those people currently driving along Morris Avenue already radicalized and plotting the deaths of countless innocent people? How would anyone know? Who would peg Michael Schuster, a middle-aged, average American salesman, as a terrorist?

She turned her back to the window, her arms hugging her

torso. "When did he first show up on your radar?"

"We've been monitoring him for the past few months. We keep an eye on anyone who rants about the government or praises various terrorist groups or other extremists on social media. Most of the time these people never take the next step, but your ex was becoming more vocal and began visiting sites known for recruiting like-minded malcontents into white nationalist militias and various foreign terrorist groups. That's when we decided to approach you."

"So, I was your insurance policy? Someone you thought could get close to him and find out what he has planned?"

Gavin nodded. "I had hoped it wouldn't come to this, but now it has. With those purchases, it's obvious Schuster has crossed the line from Internet loudmouth to terrorist and much sooner than we anticipated."

Cassandra returned to the couch and took her seat. "What do you need me to do?"

"Help us find out what he's planning and when he's planning it."

That's all? "Exactly how am I supposed to do that? With all your research on me, you must know I'm in the process of suing him over delinquent child support and alimony payments. We don't exactly get together for tea and crumpets on a weekly basis."

Gavin smiled for the first time since she'd entered his office. "I have a plan."

SEVEN

Gavin Demarco had at least one screw loose, possibly more. Cassandra stared at him in disbelief. "You want me to switch out Michael's phone? How in the world do you expect me to do that without him noticing? And even if by some chance I did pull off a slight-of-hand miracle, what happens when he notices he's got the wrong phone?"

"He won't notice."

"How could he not? What about all his apps? His contacts? His emails? His texts? They won't be on the phone I swap for his."

"They will. At least we hope so if everything works as planned."

"Hope so? Explain 'hope so.'" From where she sat this plan of Gavin's had more holes than a block of Swiss cheese. Holes that matched the ones in his head from the loose screws!

"Liam Hatch has developed a prototype smart phone that will synch up and clone the contents of a targeted phone. We'll hear every call Schuster makes and see every email and text sent and received, all in real time."

"Isn't there malware that already does that?" She remembered seeing a news article recently about spyware that could be inserted into a phone just by sending someone a text with a video link. The recipient didn't even have to click on the link for the spyware to download into the phone.

Gavin nodded. "This is different. Better. Plus, we'll be able to track his every move. The phone also contains a kill switch that will render it inoperable should he try to use it as a remote detonator."

"But not render other phones in the area inoperable?"

"Only those we target, according to Hatch."

Cassandra shuddered. "I hope he's as big a genius as you and he claim. In the wrong hands technology like that could wreak havoc."

"We're well aware of that, but we've got to get a jump on these lone wolf terrorists and militia groups. Their numbers are growing at an alarming rate, and it's only a matter of time before one of them succeeds in pulling off a massive attack, something far worse than the Boston Marathon bombings. It's imperative we use whatever technology we have at our disposal to stop them."

Cassandra felt the need to point out a lesson from history. "If I remember my honors U.S. History class senior year, that was the rationale used to drop the A-bombs on Hiroshima and Nagasaki."

Gavin steepled his fingers. The office grew silent for several beats before he answered her. "As devastating as those bombs were, don't forget they ended the war. In the long run, the decision to use them saved countless lives."

"But they also started the arms race and a nuclear proliferation we're still dealing with," she argued.

"Which would have happened anyway. It was only a matter of

time. I guarantee, the bad guys are already hard at work on a version of the same technology Liam has developed."

"I suppose that's probably true." Frightening but true.

"Anyway, this is not the time for a philosophical debate. We have a terrorist to stop."

Cassandra sighed. "You're right, of course. It just scares the hell out of me. This phone Hatch has developed, it's not totally perfected yet?"

"The technology has worked in limited trials so far. Right now it's our best plan of attack for determining what Schuster has planned."

Cassandra raised her index finger. "Here's the first flaw in your plan. I don't have a clue as to the brand of cell phone Michael owns."

"We've got that covered. Delta Team has already discovered the make and model as well as identified the type of phone case. Liam will have the phone ready by tomorrow. All we need to do is position a team member within two feet of him for ninety seconds, and the technology will do the rest."

"A team member? Not me?"

"No, someone he doesn't know. A stranger who can get close to him without arousing suspicion. Delta Team is on surveillance, monitoring his schedule."

That brought her to the second flaw in his plan. "Michael is a sales rep for a pharmaceutical company. His territory covers half of New Jersey and parts of New York, Connecticut, and Pennsylvania. He's all over the map every day, never in the same place at the same time on any given day. How are you going to pull this off? It's not like he's a cashier at a supermarket you can stand in front of while he's ringing up your order or a bus driver you can sit behind while riding into Manhattan."

"He takes customers out to lunch, doesn't he?"

"All the time."

"A member of Delta Team will be sitting at the table next to him wherever he eats lunch tomorrow."

"Assuming the tables are no more than two feet apart, then what?"

"Once we have his phone cloned, you're going to make the switch."

As serious as the discussion was, Cassandra couldn't help but laugh. "Is that all?" She threw up her arms. "Piece of cake—not! Let me remind you the man and I have barely spoken in five years."

"We're going to make certain you find a way."

She had little faith in this plan, and the more she thought about it, the bigger that block of Swiss cheese grew. "What if he uses a different phone for his terrorism connections? Don't criminals often use burner phones and swap them out regularly?"

She lived in New Jersey and read the newspaper when she had time. She knew such things didn't only occur on TV dramas and in the movies. Gang members and drug dealers employed such tactics, not to mention all the members of organized crime who call the Garden State home.

"We have no indication of that. He's been observed using only one phone, and no secondary cell signal has pinged from his location as we've tracked his movements."

"Still, he could have a secondary phone for triggering the bomb. If I were him, I'd take a page from all those drug kingpins and gangbangers and keep a stash of pre-paid phones at my disposal."

The corners of Gavin's mouth quirked upward, causing a crack in his grim demeanor. "That's why I'm glad you're working for the good guys. If he does plan to use a burner phone as a detonator, we've got that covered. The jammer on the cloned phone will also jam any other phones in the general vicinity."

"But a minute ago you said—"

"Only if we want it to."

"It's that smart?"

"It's that smart."

Gavin had a rebuttal for each of her arguments. Still, so much could go wrong. One thing was clear to her, though. Judging from what Gavin's teams had unearthed, Michael was either convinced that he'd devised a foolproof plan, or he was incredibly stupid. Knowing The Ex, her money was on the latter. And that could be even more deadly than whatever he had planned.

"Bottom line," said Gavin, "Michael Schuster is dangerous and needs to be stopped."

She nodded. "Agreed. Now tell me how you plan to transform me into Cassandradini the Magnificent."

~*~

Cassandra's head spun as she headed downstairs to meet Hawkeye for target practice. One day she's writing community theater reviews; the next, she's so far out of her league, she's playing an entirely different sport in another stadium—on a distant planet— in another galaxy. How the hell had her life plummeted down such a bizarre rabbit hole?

Michael. That's how. Because of him, she'd been sucked into this alien world of counterterrorism. Now she was charged with stopping The Ex from blowing up some unidentified target.

What on earth had Michael gotten himself mixed up in? Their years together had given no inkling that someday the average two-timing Joe would morph into a potential mass murderer. But since then? Other than his recent marriage and the impending arrival of twins—talk about irony—she knew little of the life he'd led the past five years.

Besides her lawyer, her children were her only source of news regarding Michael. They told her very little, not because they withheld information from her but because they just didn't know much.

Michael had very little contact with his children—his choice, not hers. But had it not been for Hayley and Cooper, Cassandra wouldn't have had anything to do with the lying cheat once the ink on the divorce decree had dried.

She stepped out of the elevator and found Hawkeye standing in front of the door to the firing range. He tapped the face of the high-tech watch on his wrist. "You're late."

"Blame Gavin. He called me into his office."

Hawkeye showed a concern she didn't expect. "Everything okay?"

Cassandra knew not to discuss operations with non-team members unless instructed to do so. "Hunky-dory," she said, forcing a smile.

Hawkeye keyed in the code to the firing range, then opened the door, holding it for her to proceed ahead of him. "Don't look like hunky-dory from where I'm standing." He stepped into the room and closed the door behind him. Then he nodded to the line of targets at the opposite end of the long tunnel. "Tell you what, just visualize your ex's face on those targets while you're shooting, and you'll have one hell of a practice session."

Cassandra turned to face him. Hands on hips, she scowled. "You know?"

"Hell, yeah."

He handed her what looked like the same Glock she'd used yesterday, not that she'd know one Glock from another or a Glock from a Barretta or a Walther PPK, the only other handgun names she knew from having watched a few James Bond movies back in the day.

"Why do you think I'm tasked with whipping you into shape so quickly?"

Cassandra placed the gun on the counter. "You mean you don't kill all your new recruits as quickly as you're killing me?"

Hawkeye laughed. "Turn around and shoot the head off that mother-f'er."

And she did. Cassandra was shocked at how quickly and accurately she had adapted to firing the gun after only two weeks of practice. She just hoped she'd never have to use the Glock anywhere other than the MAC basement firing range. Aiming at a paper target was one thing. Firing at another human being was something else.

Chill foreboding swept up her spine. She had accepted a job that supposedly entailed sitting at a computer all day. That job had swiftly morphed into something altogether different from the initial job description—with the potential of being far more deadly.

Given what she now knew, could she kill the father of her children if she had to?

Cassandra inserted another clip into the gun, positioned herself, and pulled the trigger. She hoped to hell she'd never have to face that possibility.

~*~

Gavin accessed the MAC closed-circuit monitoring system on his computer and intently studied Cassandra while she took target practice with Hawkeye. Her body language now exuded a determination decidedly missing from his initial session with her. After their talk yesterday she hit the kill zone with nearly every shot. So far today she hadn't missed once. Impressive.

He ignored the unwelcome hormonal elephant that had unexpectedly entered the firing range on the one and only day he'd worked with her. He chalked up her new attitude and improved performance to his revelations about her ex. Cassandra had quickly channeled her fear and anger into a focused resolve to stop a terrorist.

He'd made the right decision in turning her over to Hawkeye for her physical training. Given the stakes, he would have preferred training her himself, but the last thing he needed was his long-suppressed libido springing back to life and clouding his judgment in the middle of a crucial operation. He vowed to keep Cassandra Davenport at arm's length just in case that unexpected surge of testosterone was more a precursor of what could be rather than an anomaly.

Gavin picked up his phone and called Carla Jordan to report in on his progress.

"Glad to hear she's working out," said Carla.

Gavin knew Carla wasn't totally onboard with MAC. Each of their successes over the last six months had won her over a little bit more, but she still harbored strong reservations regarding the use of civilians and wanted them kept out of the field as much as possible.

When one of his agents had gone rogue a few weeks ago during a surveillance op and attacked a suspected terrorist, the woman had not only put the continued existence of MAC in jeopardy, she'd created a potential nightmare for Tony Granville. If the president axed Tony over a botched MAC operation, MAC died a sudden death.

Luckily, because of Carla's concerns over recruiting civilians as operatives, she'd anticipated the possibility of just such a SNAFU. She quickly launched a credible cover story that not only kept the news media at bay but prevented prosecution of the former team member. As she had done throughout much of her career, Carla Jordan once again pulled an unorthodox rabbit out of her hat. Then again, if MAC went south, Carla had as much—if not more—to lose than the rest of them. However, Gavin knew he couldn't afford any more failures within his ranks.

"We were able to clone the phone without a hitch," he continued. "Schuster never suspected a thing."

"You're all set to make the switch tomorrow?"

"Hopefully. We still need Davenport to place a call to her ex-husband to set up a meet."

"Keep me posted." Carla hung up before Gavin had a chance to say anything further.

He turned back to his computer screen to find that Cassandra had finished her target practice for the day. Time to set the next part of his plan in motion.

EIGHT

When Cassandra returned to her team, she found Gavin waiting with Noreen and Hanna. It was time for her to call Michael. "What if he refuses to meet with me?" she asked.

"That carrot you'll be dangling will do the trick," said Gavin. "Money talks."

Cassandra thought about that. "Michael always complained that we never had enough money to support the lifestyle he believed he deserved. I called it caviar dreams on a mac and cheese budget." She paused for a moment, then snapped her fingers. "Of course!"

"What?" asked Noreen.

"All of this is so not Michael. He's not building a bomb because of some sudden conversion to a radical form of Islam; he's doing it for the money. Someone is paying him."

"If he's not committed to the cause, he's in for a rude awakening," said Hanna. "An infidel is an infidel, whether he's helpful or not. These groups have no tolerance for anyone who isn't a true believer of their cause."

"Whatever the reason," said Gavin, "we have to figure out what he's planning and stop him."

Cassandra fished her personal cell phone, not her MAC-issued phone, out of her purse and took a deep breath. She then exhaled forcefully. "Okay, let's get this over with."

"Do you want to rehearse once more?" asked Hanna. The three of them had devised a script for Cassandra to follow.

"No, I've got my lines down." All those years of high school drama club had left her with the ability to memorize dialogue after only a few reads of most scripts.

"We've got your back," said Noreen. "Put the phone on speaker. We'll feed you lines if necessary. Just keep your eyes on my computer screen for any prompts."

Cassandra nodded, then scrolled through her contacts until she came to Michael's number. She paused for a split second to jack up her courage before activating the call.

"What do you want?" he asked with a snarl in his voice and not so much as a begrudging greeting.

Cassandra scowled at the phone. "Hello to you, too, Michael."

"I'm busy, Cassandra. Whatever crap you want to hurl at me today, call my lawyer."

"Actually, I'm calling to do you a favor," she said. "Or at least offer you one if you're interested."

This got his attention, but his voice sounded leery. "What sort of favor?"

She launched into her pitch. "I'm tired of fighting with you, Michael. All we're doing is making our lawyers richer. You have a new life with twins on the way. I want to get on with my life. I have a proposition that should interest you."

"What sort of proposition?"

"Meet me for lunch tomorrow. Give me an hour of your time, and you'll save thousands of dollars in legal fees."

"Why can't you just tell me over the phone?"

"I don't have time, and I think we should discuss this face-to-face."

He paused long enough that Cassandra thought he'd hung up on her. Finally, he said, "Fine. Chez Jacques at one o'clock. You're paying." Then he did hang up.

Cassandra sighed. She turned to Gavin. "Sorry. I screwed up. I should have named the restaurant before he had a chance to choose one." Gavin had made arrangements to fill a specific restaurant entirely with MAC personnel.

"Don't worry about it," he said.

"A guy like that has to throw his weight around to compensate for his own shortcomings," said Noreen. "That's why he's building a bomb. It makes him feel important and in control of the world."

"Besides," said Hanna, "even if you had suggested the restaurant we chose, he probably would've balked."

"She's right," said Gavin. "Not having total control of the restaurant is a minor glitch, but it's not a deal breaker. We can tweak our plan to fit Chez Jacques."

Cassandra snorted. "So like him to pick the most expensive restaurant in the state and stick me with the check."

"We can afford it," said Gavin. He placed a hand on her shoulder, then quickly removed it. "You did great. We proceed as planned."

He turned and strode back to his office. Cassandra was left to deal with the aftermath of the electric sizzle produced by his brief touch. *Damn!*

~*~

Cassandra arrived at the restaurant half an hour before the designated time in order to choose a table in the far corner, placing herself with her back to the wall and facing the entrance. Michael would have only her and the cabbage rose wallpaper to stare at, while she had a bird's eye view of the other diners, including the various MAC teams positioned at tables throughout the restaurant.

Gavin had made arrangements to reserve the entire restaurant for the afternoon. Along with Alpha Team, he had enlisted Sigma, Theta, and Omega, as well as a few people from IT and security to dine at Chez Jacques this afternoon.

"Why not Delta Team?" she had asked. "Isn't this their op?"

"We don't want to risk the possibility of Schuster recognizing one of them from our earlier surveillance," said Gavin. "They'll be with me in a van parked a block away. We'll be monitoring everything from there."

"How?"

"Everyone will wear cameras and earbuds."

Some team members were already in position when she arrived, including Hanna and Noreen, who were halfway through their meals. Others began streaming into the restaurant in groups of twos, threes, and fours once she'd taken her seat. All had forsaken their standard blend-into-the-background black outfits and instead wore designer suits. Dressed in Dolce & Gabbana, Chanel, and Donna Karan, the women all looked very much like well-to-do society matrons who spent their days chairing charity events, exactly the type of women who lunched at Chez Jacques on a weekday.

Cassandra had chosen to wear a gray unconstructed raw silk

jacket over a pair of black dress slacks. A daisy cloisonné lapel pin contained what appeared to be a small emerald in the center of the flower. No one would ever suspect the gemstone was actually a miniature camera. More importantly, the jacket had large, deep pockets to conceal the cloned phone, and the silk material would enable her to slip one phone out and the other into her pocket with ease. Or so she hoped.

As she sat waiting for Michael, she noticed three tables filled with diners she didn't recognize, one with four men and the other two each with a man and a woman. She assumed they were the IT and security people Gavin had mentioned.

Michael had never been on time for anything in his life, including their wedding. So Cassandra wasn't surprised that one o'clock came and went without his arrival. He finally sauntered in at one-twenty. She took note of the smug expression he wore along with the three-piece suite that fit him too well for an off-the-rack purchase. His closet probably contained a dozen more.

When he unbuttoned his suit jacket and shot his French cuffs, solid gold cufflinks with an "M" and "S" spelled out in diamond chips twinkled in the light of the overhead chandelier. His attire was a far cry from the Walmart specials he wore in front of the judge when he complained he couldn't afford the child support the court had decreed he pay.

Michael took the seat opposite her and checked his phone before placing it on the table beside his plate. *So far so good.* Delta Team had mentioned he always kept his phone on the table while eating in a restaurant. Such a habit would make the switcheroo much easier. Cassandra had no idea how she would have pulled the slight-of-hand off had he kept his phone in his pants or jacket pocket.

Michael picked up the menu and began to peruse it without a word to her. *So typical.* She kept her cool. The last thing she wanted to do was antagonize him, even though she realized he was trying his damnedest to provoke her.

The waitress arrived at their table. "Can I get you something to drink, sir?"

"Macallan on the rocks. Make it a double."

Of course he'd order the priciest Scotch on the menu. The waitress turned to Cassandra. "Anything more for you, ma'am?"

"I'm fine for now, thank you." Needing to keep her wits about her, she'd ordered a Perrier and lime earlier.

"Would you like to order now, or do you need more time?"

"I'll have the lobster," said Michael, handing the menu back to the waitress. He glanced at Cassandra, looking for a reaction, but she refused to give him the satisfaction.

The waitress turned to her. Knowing Michael expected her to order the cheapest item on the menu—not that anything could really be considered cheap at Chez Jacques—to offset the cost of his sixty-dollar lunch, she chose an entrée only slightly less expensive than his. "The crab almandine, please."

She noticed a slight downturn of his mouth, as if unhappy his choice hadn't produced the desired reaction. "Win the lottery?" he asked.

"I never play."

He fell silent until the waitress returned with his drink. After taking a sip, he smacked his lips, then asked, "So what's this proposition you have for me?"

Before Cassandra had a chance to say anything, Noreen approached their table. She glared at Michael. "I thought it was you, you bastard! How dare you get my daughter pregnant, then walk out on her?"

She grabbed the glass of Scotch out of his hand and threw the contents in his face, splattering the liquid in his eyes.

"What the f—" Michael jumped to his feet, toppling his chair backwards. "I can't see! I'm blind!" He flailed his arms, knocking into the table, causing it to teeter toward Cassandra. She slid off her chair as glasses and silverware headed for her lap, grabbing his phone as it began to slide off the table. Before Michael opened his eyes, she deftly made the switch, dropping his phone into her pocket and leaving the cloned phone in its place.

The waitress rushed over, napkins in hand, as Noreen exited the restaurant. Cassandra dipped a napkin in a glass of water and handed it to Michael. "Use this," she said.

Cursing nonstop, he dabbed at his eyes. When he was finally able to open them, he squinted around the room. "Where is that crazy bitch? Did you see what she did to me?" he asked no one in particular.

"I want her arrested for assault." He grabbed his phone. "I'm calling the police."

But Noreen was long gone, the other patrons had returned to their meals, and two busboys had arrived to clean up the mess. No one paid any attention to Michael.

Cassandra grabbed her purse and stood. Leaning over him, she sneered. "You'll never change."

"What? I have no idea who that crazy bitch was. I've never seen her before in my life."

"I stopped falling for your lies a long time ago, Michael. I'm certainly not falling for them now." She turned to leave.

He grabbed for her arm, but she stepped out of his reach. "Where are you going? What about this deal you had for me?"

"I changed my mind. I'll see you in court." Chin raised, she strode toward the door.

"Get back here. You're paying for this meal."

Cassandra kept walking but called over her shoulder, "I changed my mind about that, too."

She exited the restaurant, and rushed down the street, hoping he hadn't decided to follow her. At the corner she turned into a municipal parking lot and headed for a navy blue commercial van lettered *Johnson Brothers Plumbing & Supply Co.* The rear door opened for her before she had a chance to reach for the handle.

"Nice job," said Gavin after she stepped into the air-conditioned truck. He closed the door behind her.

"You can breathe again," said Noreen.

She chuckled. "Good to know. Thanks." As nervous as she'd been about this operation, it had gone off without a hitch—just as Gavin had predicted. She reached into her jacket pocket, retrieved Michael's phone, and handed it to him. Then she removed the earbud and pin and handed them to Noreen.

Two long counters ran the length of the vehicle behind the driver and passenger seats. Keyboards lined the counters. Wall-mounted computer monitors hung above each station. Along with Noreen and Gavin, the three members of Delta Team, all wearing headphones, sat next to each other on one side. All had turned to nod at her when she entered the van. One Mom, a woman named Allison, gave her a thumbs-up.

"What did he do after I left?" asked Cassandra. She had thought Michael might race after her and try to drag her back to the restaurant.

"See for yourself," said one of the other Delta Moms. She pressed a few keys, then pointed to the monitor in front of her.

Cassandra watched as Michael, his eyes bloodshot and his bespoke suit and shirt spotted with expensive Scotch, stormed toward her departing back. As he passed Hanna's table, she moved her foot ever so slightly to the side, tripping him. He landed flat on his face.

"Ouch! I don't suppose he paid the bill."

"By the time he picked himself up and started ranting about lawsuits, the restaurant was just happy to see him leave," said the third Delta Mom.

"We've already taken care of the bill," said Gavin.

"Too bad we couldn't get his lobster as take-out," said Cassandra. She hadn't eaten anything since seven o'clock that morning. It was now nearly two o'clock. A hunger headache had gathered at her temples and her stomach rumbled from neglect.

Gavin chuckled, then winked at her as a flush of embarrassment rose up her neck and spread across her face. When she noticed the Delta moms staring at her, the heat in her cheeks intensified. She quickly shifted her stance to turn her back on them.

Gavin hadn't noticed. Or if he had, he pretended not to. He continued without missing a beat. "What makes you think we didn't? I also ordered lobsters for Delta Team and myself. Hanna will bring everything back to the office."

NINE

While Gavin, Cassandra, and the Delta moms feasted on lobster in the cafeteria, Gavin tasked Noreen and Hanna with searching Schuster's phone for anything that would give them an inkling of his target and the timeframe for carrying out his attack.

"Anything?" he asked when he and Cassandra joined them later.

"Nothing beyond what we already know from monitoring his social media postings," said Hanna, "but at this point we've just made a cursory pass through his calendar, emails, and texts."

"He doesn't appear to have any friends," said Noreen.

"Typical of a lone wolf," said Gavin.

Noreen continued, "He doesn't communicate with anyone other than clients, business associates, and his wife. His calendar is filled mostly with sales calls, except for a number of doctor appointments. The calendar doesn't list names or locations for those, though. They're simply marked *dr*."

"His wife is in her third trimester with twins," said Cassandra.

"Although, I can't say he ever accompanied me to any of my OB appointments."

"Guys always lavish more attention on the trophy wife," said Hanna.

"Look into it," Gavin told Noreen, "then start digging deeper. There's got to be something we're missing."

"What would you like me to do?" asked Cassandra.

"I want to know everything you know about this new wife of his," he said.

Cassandra shrugged. "Not much."

"Let's sit down and talk about it. You probably know more than you realize." Gavin moved to place his hand on the small of her back to lead her to his office but quickly dropped his arm to his side before he touched her. When he'd briefly placed his hand on her shoulder earlier, he knew instantly he'd made a mistake. He couldn't afford to let temptation get the better of him. With each passing day his attraction to her grew, despite doing everything in his power to ensure otherwise.

Instead, they walked side by side down the corridor with plenty of room between them. He opened his office door, and Cassandra preceded him inside. She walked across the room to the seating area and settled onto the sofa. Gavin grabbed the chair opposite her. "We haven't been able to find out much about Schuster's wife," he said, "other than some basic details."

"What have you learned?"

He rose and retrieved a file from the top of his desk, handing it to her after he returned to his chair. The file contained only two sheets of paper, one with notes and the other a surveillance photo of Michael and his wife shot by Delta Team.

He waited while Cassandra perused the minimal amount of

data. Her mouth dropped open, and she raised her head to look at him. "She's a doctor?"

"Of psychology, not medicine."

She shook her head. "I figured he met her at Hooters. That's where he used to troll for fresh conquests when we were married." She dropped her head again and continued reading. "He's way out of her league. What the hell does she see in him?"

"You tell me."

She snorted. "I haven't a clue. Michael is no catch by any stretch of the imagination, at least not for someone with these credentials. His parents wanted him to go to med school, but thanks to spending more time partying than studying, he barely squeaked through college. Needless to say, he never got into med school."

When Gavin raised an eyebrow, she quickly added, "No, I didn't know him back then. We met after I graduated. He was already working."

"As a sales rep?"

"The pre-med courses he took gave him enough knowledge to score a job in the pharmaceutical industry. He's also got the perfect talent for a job in sales."

"What's that?"

"When motivated, he oozes charm by the barrel. Some people go through life on their brains, others on their talent, and still others on their looks; Michael employs charm. If he wants something, he has a knack for manipulating people—especially women—into giving him what he wants. It makes him a very successful salesman."

She scowled. "However, it's all a game to him, and once he gets what he wants, he moves on. The conquest is all that counts."

She focused back on the photo. "What he usually wants, though, are big-breasted dumb blondes just shy of jailbait."

He studied her for a moment. "Forgive me for saying this, but—"

She glanced down at her so-not-a-Double-D chest, then back at him. "I'm neither? Funny, isn't it? I guess it's the Madonna/Whore complex prevalent in some men."

She tapped the photo. "This Double-D doesn't exactly fit the mold—except for the Double-D part."

"Double-D?"

Cassandra blushed. "Sorry. That's what I call her, what I've called all of them. Believe it or not, up to this moment, I didn't know her name."

Gavin nodded. Even though Jane Smith wore large sunglasses and a floppy straw hat in the photo, it was clear to see she was definitely no blonde. Wavy jet-black hair fell across her shoulders. According to Delta Team, Jane always wore large hats and dark glasses out in public. Even when only a few feet away from her, they couldn't tell if Jane had an olive complexion, spent hours in a tanning salon, or was of mixed race. However, at thirty-five she was definitely a far cry from jailbait.

"They must have met on the job," said Cassandra. "Glenmeade Pharmaceuticals is the same company where Michael works, although he's rarely in the office."

"Anything stand out to you?" asked Gavin. He studied Cassandra's body language. She reacted with cool objectivity to the information he'd presented her. Outwardly she showed no animosity toward Michael's new wife. Since she and Michael had divorced five years ago, he doubted Jane Smith was the other woman at the time of their divorce.

Cassandra returned the papers to the folder and placed the folder on the coffee table. "Aside from wondering what she sees in Michael and why a pharmaceutical company would employ a psychologist?"

He nodded.

"Her name for starters. Jane Smith? It might as well be Jane Doe."

"Anything else?"

She leaned forward and tapped the folder. "What's even odder is that this is all you've been able to find out about her. Where was she born? Where has she lived? Where did she go to school? Where else has she worked? What about relatives?" She leaned back and folded her arms across her chest. "There's nothing here. With all the available tech you have at your disposal, this is all anyone could uncover about her?"

"Odd isn't it? We've been trying to find out more, but we've hit a brick wall. It's possible she testified against someone and was placed in WITSEC. Tony's looking into that angle, but the U.S. Marshals are averse to divulging such information."

"Even to the Attorney General?"

"To anyone. It's part of the pact they make with people who agree to enter the program. The marshals are charged with keeping them safe. They don't want any leaks that could place those under their protection in jeopardy."

"I don't think that's her real name."

He raised an eyebrow. "Really?"

"I guess you already figured that one out, huh?"

He chuckled. "The thought had occurred to me. What else can you tell me?"

Cassandra shrugged. "I've never actually met her. She hasn't accompanied Michael to court, and when he remembers to exercise his visitation privileges, either he picks the kids up, or I drop them off, but I always stay in the car. I've never been inside their house." She retrieved the photo from the folder and held it up. "This is the first I've seen her other than catching an occasional quick glimpse from a distance. Not that this photo really tells us anything. The sunglasses hide her eyes, and given the angle of the photo, the brim of the hat covers much of her face. Delta Team couldn't get a better shot?"

"This was the best of the lot. What about your kids? Have they mentioned anything?"

"They've said she generally isn't home when they visit. When she is, she has very little to do with them and insists they refer to her as Mrs. Schuster. They've told me they spend most of their visits in the den in front of the television until it's time to return home."

She pulled a frown. "Michael lacks even the most basic of parenting skills, and if Jane Smith has any maternal instincts, she's reserving them for her own kids."

Gavin leaned forward and frowned at her. He heaved a grunt, then asked the one question he'd wanted to ask her from the moment they met. "Why the hell did you marry this guy?"

"Because we all make mistakes in life?" She sighed. "Like most manipulative bastards, he's got a Dr. Jekyll/Mr. Hyde personality. Mr. Hyde didn't show up until a few years after the 'I do's'—once the kids were born and he had responsibilities thrust upon him. Turns out Michael doesn't do responsibility well.

"It was downhill after that. Affairs that he'd deny at first. Every time I'd threaten to leave, Dr. Jekyll would suddenly reappear and promise to change. And he would—for a few months. Then Mr.

Hyde would show up again. I finally had enough of the roller coaster ride and called it quits."

"How did he take it?"

"Not well. Michael likes being in control. He also doesn't like spending money on anyone but himself. Now he's got alimony and child support payments, which are frequently delinquent. Ever since he remarried, he's even more delinquent. I finally filed contempt charges, and my lawyer is going to request wage garnishment at the next hearing. That's really going to set him off."

Gavin leaned back and steepled his fingers under his chin. "I've been thinking about what you said regarding his motives. You could be right, that he's doing this for the money and not because of some newfound religious or political fanaticism."

"Trust me, he's definitely doing this for money. Anything Michael does, he does for money. If he's in the process of planning a massive terrorist attack, it's not over some newfound ideology; it's because someone promised him several million dollars to blow something or someone up."

~*~

Alpha and Delta Teams spent the next several days getting nowhere. Not only had Michael's phone so far not yielded any secrets, monitoring his conversations had also revealed no useful information.

Gavin held a briefing with the two teams in the third-floor conference room. Alpha Team sat on one side of the table, Delta Team across from them, and Gavin at the head. No one looked happy.

"It's almost as if he knows he's being monitored," said Hanna.

"His silence certainly speaks volumes," added Allison, the

Delta Mom who had given Cassandra the thumbs-up sign days before after she'd switched the phones.

Stunned, Cassandra's jaw dropped. "You can't possibly think—"

"What else should we think?" added one of the other Delta Moms, a woman named Esther. "The guy and his wife hardly speak to each other. Don't you think that's pretty odd behavior for a recently married couple, especially a couple expecting twins? Not only aren't we picking up on anything useful, we're hardly even hearing any mundane chitchat, just mostly the television blaring."

"Which is probably done to mask their real conversations," said Virginia, the third member of Delta Team.

"They're acting like they know their house is bugged," said Esther. "Someone had to have tipped him off."

"Maybe he's paranoid and just being overly cautious," said Cassandra. "Maybe his wife has no clue what he's up to, maybe—"

"Maybe we've got ourselves a mole," said Allison staring pointedly at her.

The two other Delta Moms also glared at her with equally accusatory expressions. Cassandra glanced at Noreen and Hanna, but they had both averted their eyes.

"You all saw and heard what happened at the restaurant," she said. "You know I didn't tip him off."

"Doesn't mean you didn't do it at some other point," said Virginia.

Cassandra fought back tears. How could they possibly think she was complicit in a terrorist plot? She turned to Gavin. "Is that what you think, too?"

Instead of answering her, his gaze swept across the table, capturing the attention of each of the other Moms. "I won't have wild speculation setting you against one another. There is no place in this organization for catty schoolgirl behavior."

"You've tasked us with thinking outside the box," said Allison. "You have to consider all possibilities."

Gavin nodded. "Yes, I do. You have a case to make, act like the professionals you're supposed to be. Bring me proof, not accusations based on wild speculation."

"Did it ever occur to you," said Esther, "that a bit of wild speculation on the part of Alpha Team might have prevented—"

"We had no way of knowing that would happen," said Noreen, glaring across the table.

"Maybe you should have," said Virginia.

Gavin slammed his hand on the table. "Enough!" He stood and walked toward the door. Before leaving the room, he turned back to them. "All of you get back to work. We have a terrorist to stop. If you can't work together and focus on the job, get the hell out of here."

He slammed the door behind him. As soon as Gavin departed, Delta Team rose as one. Avoiding eye contact with Alpha Team and saying not a word, they exited behind Gavin.

Hanna placed her hand on Cassandra's forearm. "I'm sorry. I didn't mean to suggest you had anything to do with this."

"They came with an agenda," added Noreen.

Cassandra nodded to acknowledge their comments but didn't say anything. She needed to get away from all of them before she broke down and made a fool of herself. "I need some air," she finally said and made a beeline for the door.

"Would you like some company?" Hanna called after her.

Cassandra shook her head as she closed the door behind her.

~*~

Damn! The last thing Gavin needed was a rift between his teams. He wanted to throttle all three Delta members. They'd obviously orchestrated this attack against Cassandra ahead of time. *But why?* Because their search to uncover Schuster's plan had so far failed? What kind of crap was that, trying to plant doubt about Cassandra in his mind? She was no more to blame for their lack of success than he was.

He swung open the fire door at the end of the corridor and stormed downstairs to the basement gym. Once inside he threw the interior door bolt and disabled the camera feed. At the far end of the gym he stripped off his clothes, tossing them aside. Naked, he attacked a hundred-pound bag with his bare knuckles.

Right cross. Left hook. Right cross. Over and over Gavin pounded the hell out of the bag. Sweat stung his eyes and poured down his body, spraying across the floor as he continued to assault the bag, swinging left, right, left. Jab. Cross. Hook. Uppercut. Jab. Cross. Hook. Uppercut. He kept at it for ten, fifteen, twenty minutes, finally collapsing in a heap on the sweat-slickened floor after thirty minutes.

Too spent to move, he lay there on his back for several minutes, one arm draped across his forehead, forcing air into his lungs. Still angry.

After about five minutes he leveraged himself to his feet, grabbed his clothes and headed into the locker room to shower. When he returned to the gym, he found Hawkeye mopping up his sweat. "How the hell did you get in? I bolted the door."

Hawkeye nodded toward the office. "Been here the whole time. Haven't seen you pummel a bag like that in ages. Not since back in our Corps days."

Gavin grunted.

"You need to get yourself laid, man."

"You need to mind your own business."

Hawkeye shrugged. "Just saying. It ain't natural."

"Neither is veganism. When was the last time you sank your teeth into a good steak?"

Hawkeye leaned on the mop handle and considered the question. "Around about the last time you sank your—"

Gavin was out the door before Hawkeye finished his sentence. He didn't need sex; he needed to bring down terrorists. Besides, he'd tried the no-strings-attached route. It gave him about as much pleasure as his own hand. He'd rather do without. Celibacy wasn't so bad once you got used to it. Or so he kept telling himself.

Deciding to let Delta Team stew for a bit, he headed back upstairs to talk to Alpha Team. "Where's Cassandra?" he asked as he approached Noreen and Hanna.

"She left," said Noreen.

"What do you mean?"

"She was really upset," said Hanna. "Said she had to get some air and walked out nearly an hour ago. She hasn't returned."

"This day keeps getting better and better," muttered Gavin.

"Anything you want us to do?" asked Noreen.

"Discover Schuster's plan."

"Working on it."

"Work faster."

Gavin headed back to his office to grab his jacket. On the way he consulted the app on his phone that gave him the location of all his team members. The GPS showed Cassandra at home. Had she decided to quit, taking the coward's way out by not even telling him to his face?

She didn't strike him as a quitter. However, he'd been surprised that she hadn't stood up for herself more against Delta Team's accusations. Instead she'd tucked tail and slinked off to lick her wounds. But she'd taken her MAC phone with her instead of leaving it at the office. This gave him hope that maybe she did just need a bit of space and time to regroup.

He needed her. Cassandra Davenport was their best hope at stopping her lunatic ex-husband from whatever attack he was planning. Gavin didn't want to lose her—for that reason and if he were being honest with himself, another he tried to block from his mind. She'd awakened feelings he'd thought long dead.

TEN

Cassandra looked through the front door peephole to find Gavin standing on her porch. He might not be the last man on the planet she wanted to see right now, but he ran a close second. Reluctantly, she swung open the door. They stared at each other for a long moment. Finally, Gavin said, "I don't remember giving you the rest of the day off."

"I don't stay where I'm not wanted."

"Who said you're not wanted?"

"You didn't exactly stand up for me earlier."

"You didn't exactly stand up for yourself."

"I tried."

"Hardly."

"So that makes me guilty?"

"No, it makes you a coward."

"Good to know."

She started to close the door on him, but he grabbed it out of her hand. "Are you going to invite me in, or should we stand here and let all the heat escape from your house? If you're quitting, you need to think about saving money, not wasting it."

She exhaled a huff of annoyance. "Fine. Come inside if that's what you want." She turned and walked toward the living room. Behind her she heard him close the front door and follow her.

Cassandra positioned herself in front of the fireplace, her hands on her hips. She watched as Gavin scoped out the room, his gaze moving from the Oriental rug covering a portion of the hardwood floor, to the seating area flanking the fireplace, to the dining room beyond. Without being invited, he took a seat on one of the two facing sofas separated by a matching upholstered ottoman.

"Why are you here?" she asked.

"I think that's obvious."

She didn't want to play games, not with him or anyone else. She walked over to the sofa opposite him and sat. "You led me to believe everyone at MAC worked together. Delta blindsided me. All of a sudden I was back in junior high, the new kid surrounded by bullies on the playground."

"Why didn't you stand your ground?"

"Why didn't you defend me?"

"I did."

"No, you told them to bring you proof instead of hurling accusations. There's a big difference."

Gavin ran his hands through his hair and blew out a breath. "I knew they wouldn't find any proof."

"I didn't know that. From where I sat you acknowledged the possibility that I could be a mole. I can't work for someone who doesn't trust me."

"I trust you."

"You should have told them."

Gavin leaned forward and rested his forearms on his thighs. "Look, everyone is hyper-tense and frustrated. We thought once we had switched the phones, we'd discover a goldmine of information that would enable us to take Schuster down immediately."

"But it hasn't worked out that way, and for some reason I'm being blamed for your lack of progress," she said.

"You're not being blamed."

"Could've fooled me. I felt like a sacrificial lamb at that meeting. Delta Team isn't gathering any useful intel from their eavesdropping, so it must be the new kid's fault."

"They were wrong to jump to that conclusion."

"And you were wrong not to defend me."

"You're right. I should have silenced them immediately. I'm sorry."

She leaned back and folded her arms across her chest. "I don't know that I can work with people who suspect me of some ulterior motive, especially in something as nefarious as terrorism."

"I understand, but I need you."

"No, you don't. I made the switch. I'm really not of any further use to you."

"That's not true. You know Schuster better than any of us. We still have no idea what he's up to. We don't even know if he's built the bomb yet, much less where he plans to set it off or when. Are the materials stored in his house? Elsewhere? Was he only a pawn who was used to purchase the materials for someone else? Is that person calling the shots?"

"You've been following him. You should know something by now."

"Following him has gotten us nowhere. We've come up empty from every angle—the surveillance, his texts and emails, his calendar, even the bug in his phone. That bomb could already be in position, and we're no closer to finding out a damn thing about it. We don't know if he's targeting a shopping mall, a movie theater, a police station, or a school. He could have his sights set on something even bigger. Innocent lives are at stake, and right now we're impotent to protect them."

"Maybe it's time to call in the FBI or Homeland Security."

"We can't. We have nothing to give them. They'd be just as powerless to stop him."

She knew all of this, and she was just as worried as Gavin and the rest of MAC. All that really mattered was preventing another terrorist attack. She owed that to her father, her brother, and all the other victims of terrorism. By running off and sulking she had acted as immature as the Mean Girls of Delta Team. She needed to swallow her pride and go back to work. "You've made your point. What more do you need me to do?"

"Get inside his house."

And she thought his last idea was loony tunes! Then again, thanks to Gavin's last plan, she had switched out Michael's phone without him suspecting anything.

"Assuming we can pull this off, then what?"

"We search for the information we need to stop him. Details have to exist somewhere, either on paper or stored on a computer."

Cassandra frowned. "I'm no lawyer, but I have seen enough cop dramas to know evidence found during an illegal search is inadmissible in court."

"True. If we find a bomb, we'll call in an anonymous tip from a burner phone, but I'm hoping we don't find one."

"Why? I thought we wanted to stop him from carrying out his plan."

"Finding a bomb in that house will only net us Schuster. The Internet makes it very easy for any fool to build incendiary devices. I want the mastermind who tasked that fool. Your ex has all the markings of a lone wolf. However, all lone wolves are really nothing more than puppets. Someone else pulls the strings, setting them on their path to destruction, whether by incendiary videos and social media postings or face-to-face contact.

"In your ex-husband's case, I don't believe his conversion occurred merely through Internet videos and Twitter feeds. We need to take down the puppet master. If not, he'll just recruit more puppets."

"You think this puppet master is here in the States, not someone in the Middle East or elsewhere?"

"I do. The more I think about it, the more sense it makes, especially if you're right about Schuster's involvement being purely for money."

"It has to be. I can't see Michael unfurling a prayer rug and prostrating himself to pray to Allah several times a day. In the time he's been under surveillance, have you ever found him anywhere near a mosque?"

"Not once."

Cassandra stood. It was time to get back to work. "I suppose you have a plan for getting us into Michael's McMansion?"

He grinned. "Naturally."

~*~

Cassandra had to admit Gavin's plan was pure genius. Of course, it helped to have friends in high places, friends who could stage a fake gas leak—no questions asked—that necessitated the evacuation of several square blocks of homes.

Carla Jordan had called in favors of her own, securing the help of some of her former team members to pose as gas company emergency crews and outfitting vehicles to masquerade as those from the utility company. Any calls from the residents in the area to 911 or the gas company were immediately intercepted and rerouted to Noreen and Hanna, posing as operators.

No one had mentioned anything to her, but Cassandra suspected Delta Team knew nothing about tonight's operation. She hadn't seen any of the three women since they walked out of the conference room after accusing her of being a mole. For all she knew, Gavin had canned the lot of them, but she decided not to raise the subject, not with him nor with Noreen or Hanna. She figured she'd find out eventually. Right now, Delta Team was the least of her worries.

To play up the urgency of the situation, the fake workers first secretly released gas canisters throughout the upscale Millburn neighborhood to saturate the air with a heavy gas odor. Two work crews had cordoned off the area surrounding the manholes at either end of Michael's street, pretending to be working on the problem.

Michael and his new wife lived on a street of ten newly built homes, one more ostentatious than the next and all at least three times the size of Cassandra's Craftsman bungalow. From a location several blocks away she and Gavin sat in the Johnson Brothers Plumbing & Supply Co. commercial van, monitoring the crews' progress on a video feed.

Dressed as other gas workers, Carla's people raced from house to house, banging on doors to evacuate residents, giving them no time to grab any belongings. Few residents argued once they heard the entire neighborhood could blow at any moment. People were herded down the block where gas company buses waited to transport them to a safe location until the source of the leak had been identified and contained.

Gavin had chosen to execute the operation late in the evening, waiting until after Michael and Jane Smith arrived home. He wanted them trapped on one of those buses where his people could keep an eye on them while he and Cassandra searched their house.

Not knowing how long the operation would take, Gavin made arrangements for one of the Sigma Moms to spend the night at Cassandra's home. Hayley and Cooper were told she had an unexpected business trip. The kids had balked that they were too old for a babysitter, but she wasn't about to leave them alone overnight.

"They're about to knock on Michael's door," said Cassandra as two workers approached the house. Gavin pulled his attention from one of the other feeds and positioned himself behind her, looking over her shoulder at the monitor.

She pushed a button on the keyboard, sending the audio from the listening device in Michael's cloned phone to the computer's speaker. As she and Gavin watched the bogus gas company worker bang on the door, they heard Michael mutter, "Who the hell is that?"

"How should I know? Go answer it."

A moment later the front door of the faux French chateau swung open and Michael asked, "What do you want?"

"We need to evacuate the property, sir. There's a gas leak."

"What gas leak? I didn't hear anything on the news about a gas leak."

"You can't smell it?" asked the second worker.

Michael sniffed. "So fix it. Why do we have to leave?"

Cassandra rolled her eyes. "What a clueless idiot."

"We'll fix it as soon as we find the source, sir," said the first man. "Meanwhile, the entire area could blow at any moment. You need to leave. Now!" He grabbed Michael's arm and pulled him out of the house.

Michael dug in his heels. "I need my things."

"No time," said the worker, holding fast to Michael. "Anyone else in the house?"

"My wife."

"I'll get her," said the second worker. "You head to the bus with him." He entered the house and because he, too, wore a listening device, Cassandra and Gavin heard Jane say, "I have to get my key to lock the door."

"We need the houses unlocked in case the source of the leak is in one of them," said the man.

"But—"

"Lady, don't argue with me," he yelled as he hustled her outside. "We've got a serious situation here, and the sooner I get you to safety, the sooner I can keep your house and everyone else's from going ka-boom."

"Oscar-worthy performance," said Cassandra.

"They don't call him Brando for nothing," said Gavin.

"Brando?"

"As in Marlon. For his movie star good looks and acting chops."

Twenty minutes later Gavin heard from Hanna. "The last bus just pulled out. Power's been cut to disable home surveillance cameras. The alarm companies were notified of the gas leak and told the police are already on scene, so they don't need to notify them. You're good to go."

Cassandra and Gavin inserted earbuds to stay in touch with the other two members of Alpha Team once they left the van. Then under the cover of darkness they made their way to Michael's house and slipped inside. Maglites in hand, they checked out the first room.

"This place doesn't even look like it's ever been used," said Cassandra, noting the sparse furnishings of the living room—a sofa, one chair, and a coffee table. No knickknacks. No pictures on the walls. No books or family photos on the floor-to-ceiling built-in shelving that flanked the fireplace.

"First do a cursory sweep of each room," said Gavin. He reached into his pocket and pulled out two pairs of rubber gloves. Handing one pair to Cassandra, he said, "Wear these, and take care not to disturb anything. Let me know if something stands out as unusual. I'm going in search of their computers."

Cassandra walked from room to room, checking closets and opening drawers and cabinets. She even got down on her hands and knees, sweeping the flashlight under the one bed in the home, a king in the master bedroom. What she didn't find told her much more than anything she discovered.

She found Gavin in a downstairs office where he was downloading the contents of two laptops onto jump drives. "Something is very odd," she said.

He looked up. "What did you find?"

"It's what I didn't find that's interesting. Jane Smith is eight months pregnant with twins; yet, there's no evidence in this house of a woman about to give birth. No decorated nursery. No cribs waiting to be assembled. No car seats. No layettes. No diapers.

Nothing."

"Maybe they haven't gotten around to it yet. Some people are superstitious about buying baby things before the birth."

Not the sort of trivia most men would know. Cassandra couldn't see Gavin's expression in the dark, and she didn't dare shine the Maglite on him. Questions about his deceased wife and children swam in her head, but she refrained from asking them.

Not my place.

And definitely the wrong time for such a discussion. Then again, there would probably never be a right time for a discussion like that between the two of them. Instead she said, "I suppose."

"Did you check the garage and basement? They could have all the baby paraphernalia piled up somewhere else."

"Not yet but there's more."

Gavin removed the jump drive and powered down the first computer. "I'm listening."

"When I saw no evidence of an impending birth, I did a bit more digging. I couldn't find a single bottle of prenatal vitamins anywhere, not in the bathroom, bedroom, or kitchen. I even checked the purse sitting on the kitchen island. Doesn't it seem odd to you that a well-educated pregnant woman wouldn't know to take prenatal vitamins? Michael's phone calendar listed a number of doctor's appointments, so she's obviously under a doctor's care."

"Maybe those appointments weren't for her. What if he's seeing a doctor for some reason?"

She shrugged. "Michael is a bit of a hypochondriac. By the way, I also checked her wallet for ID. She's Jane Smith on everything—driver's license, insurance card, credit cards."

"As I expected. Someone who's gone to such lengths to hide

her past wouldn't slip up by carrying ID in her real name. Snap a picture of her driver's license so we have a better picture of her."

"Already done. She looks like she might have Mediterranean ancestry. Or even Middle Eastern. Either way, she certainly doesn't look like a Smith. Maybe she tells people she was adopted."

"Interesting. Text the photo to Noreen. Maybe we can get a hit off the facial recognition software. Up until now Delta Team hasn't been able to get a shot where she's not wearing large hats and glasses. We didn't have enough markers. Did you notice her phone anywhere?"

"No, she must have it on her."

"Check the basement and garage for the chemicals. As soon as I finish here, we'll start a more thorough search of each room, but hopefully, everything we need is on one of these computers."

Cassandra headed through the kitchen into the combination laundry room/mudroom. She opened the door to the three-car garage and gasped. Then she raced back to the office. "You've got to come see what I found in the garage."

ELEVEN

Gavin followed Cassandra back through the house to the door that led to the attached garage. She stepped aside and aimed her light into the darkness, exposing a UPS truck. "This explains why they park on their driveway instead of in their three-car garage," she said. "I'm guessing we're looking at how Michael plans to deliver the bomb."

Gavin stepped into the garage, slid open the driver's side door, and hoisted himself into the truck. A second later he stepped back out. "It's empty. Have you checked the basement yet?"

"No, I'll do that now."

"Noreen, are you hearing this? Find out if any UPS trucks have been stolen recently."

Cassandra headed down to the basement, returning a few minutes later. She found Gavin crawling out from under the truck. He stood up and brushed his hands together. "I hid a tracking device where no one will notice it even if the truck is up on a lift. Find anything in the basement?"

"Nothing."

"Any indication of recent activity down there?"

"You mean like an assembly line of yellow minions building bombs? Don't you think I would have mentioned that right off the bat?"

Gavin grunted. "I meant residue from building one—stains on the floor from spills, empty containers of drain cleaner, bleach, and acetone?"

Cassandra shook her head. "That basement doesn't look like anyone has ever set foot in it. There's nothing down there except bare cinderblock walls, a pristine concrete floor, and a few cobwebs in the corners and hanging from the rafters. If he's already built the bomb, my guess is he didn't do it here."

"And we haven't observed him anywhere else that could serve as a staging area." Gavin smacked his hand against the side of the truck. "Damn!"

"There's got to be something on their computers. Did you hear back from Noreen?"

"I told her not to bother. I already know the answer." He swung his flashlight into the far corner of the garage to expose an empty five-gallon can of brown paint and an industrial paint sprayer.

"He had to get the truck from somewhere," said Cassandra, "whether he bought it or stole it. Can you run the VIN?"

"Sure, if I had one. Someone removed them. I doubt that would help us anyway."

Cassandra lowered herself onto the steps leading down from the laundry room and placed a hand over her mouth to stifle a yawn. Although physically exhausted, her mind continued at breakneck speed. The discovery of the UPS truck put an entirely new spin on their investigation. "Jane is part of this. She has to be."

Gavin joined her on the step. "No doubt about it. Kind of hard to explain having a fake UPS truck in your garage."

"You've had Michael under surveillance but what about Jane? Has Delta Team kept tabs on her?"

Gavin cursed under his breath. "They didn't see any reason to. She never popped up trolling any pro-jihadist, foreign extremist, or white supremacist sites and never made any comments on social media that would lead them to suspect her of any involvement."

"Maybe not as Jane Smith, but I doubt that's her real name. If we knew her true identity, we'd probably find something. I think Jane's the one cooking up the bomb somewhere, not Michael."

Gavin rose and began pacing in the small area between the steps and the UPS truck. "If so, she's nuts. The woman is eight months pregnant. Those bombs are extremely unstable. What woman in her right mind would jeopardize her unborn children in that way?"

"Who said she's in her right mind? Besides, based on the lack of anything baby-related in this house, I'm beginning to think she's not really pregnant. Or if she and Michael are even married. I didn't find a single wedding photo in the house. How many married couples don't have a wedding portrait on display somewhere in their home?"

"An interesting observation," said Gavin, "but we know a marriage license was filed in Essex County."

"Which might be a fake, along with all of Jane's ID. Or maybe the marriage is somehow tied to the terrorism." She grew silent for a moment, then said, "Here's what I think: Jane Smith might very well be the puppet master you're searching for."

"I have to agree with Cassandra on this," said Noreen from her monitoring position at headquarters.

"And the two of you are basing all of this on not finding any pregnancy vitamins in the house?"

"That and a few other things," said Cassandra. "Like the fact that with all the toys you have at your disposal, no one can find much of anything about Jane Smith. Everyone has a past, Gavin. Why can't we uncover hers?"

"Unless she's really in WITSEC," said Noreen, "which I'm beginning to doubt."

"Ditto," said Cassandra.

"I'm running the facial recognition program," said Noreen. "Hopefully, we'll get a hit."

"Maybe you should hand Delta Team their walking papers and let Cassandra head up a new team," said Hanna, contributing to the conversation for the first time. "As far as this particular threat goes, she's contributed more in a few days than they have in several months of monitoring Michael Schuster."

Still angry with Delta Team, Cassandra silently agreed with Hanna but instead only said, "Beginner's luck."

"Let's not forget Delta Team did identify the initial threat," said Gavin.

"And have contributed little else since," said Hanna.

"Other than accuse Cassandra of being a mole," said Noreen.

"All right," said Gavin. "Let's table the discussion about Delta Team for now. We have more pressing matters that need our attention."

He returned to the step, took hold of Cassandra's elbow, and drew her to her feet. "Not bad deductive reasoning. This is why I hired you."

"Too bad we waited so long," said Hanna. "We'd already have

those two behind bars by now."

"And be deep into tracking the next threat," said Noreen.

Cassandra wondered if there would ever come a time when there wouldn't be a next threat. Every day more and more disaffected youths around the world, especially in America, were being wooed into the clutches of madmen who convinced them to commit gruesome murders in the name of a twisted ideology. Then there were the losers, like her ex-husband, who blamed everyone but themselves for their lack of success and committed heinous crimes to get even. She sighed.

"Something wrong?" asked Gavin.

"Just a bit overwhelmed by what we've discovered. Up until now part of me hoped you'd be proven wrong. After all, Michael's still the father of my children. Now there's no denying his involvement in something sinister. Suddenly it's no longer abstract. It's all too real."

"I know it sucks, but we've got a lot of work to do yet tonight. You're not going to fade on me, are you?"

"Don't worry. No one wants him nailed more than I do."

Together she and Gavin did a more thorough search of each room but found no other evidence. Then they backtracked to make sure everything in the house was left the way they'd found it. Before leaving the property to make their way to the van, Gavin attached a tracker to the undercarriage of Jane's car.

Once they returned to the van he contacted Noreen again. "We're heading out. Wait ten minutes, then reestablish the power and have Carla's team bring home all the residents. You and Hanna go home. First thing tomorrow I want the two of you coordinating surveillance on Jane Smith. Cassandra and I will head back and start digging through the files I downloaded from the computers."

"I guess we're pulling an all-nighter?" said Cassandra.

"We have no choice. With that truck painted and ready to go, they could set their plan in motion at any moment. We still don't know if they've already built the bomb and what or who they plan to target."

"What some people won't do for paid health insurance," she muttered under her breath. "You better have lots of coffee. At some point my adrenaline is going to need a surge of caffeine to keep going."

Gavin chuckled. "I'll gladly brew you a pot from my private stash of Kona beans."

~*~

After arriving back at MAC headquarters, Gavin first stopped in the IT department located behind one of the unmarked locked rooms in the basement. He grabbed two laptops, then led Cassandra up to his third-floor apartment.

Once inside, he handed her the computers and the jump drives. "You start downloading the files; I'll start the coffee."

She glanced around the large room, an open concept living area with a small, ultra-modern kitchen at one end with sleek ebony cabinets, marble countertops, and marble subway tile backsplash. A marble-topped island with two black leather upholstered barstools separated the kitchen from the living space. At the far end of the room an open door led to a bedroom.

She bypassed the stools and walked over to a black leather sectional positioned opposite a wall of ebony built-in shelves and cabinetry that matched the modern kitchen cabinets. The largest flat screen TV she'd ever seen hung between the floor-to-ceiling bookcases. Myriad high-tech electronics equipment filled the shelves under the television. Cassandra assumed the system was much more than just an entertainment unit.

She nodded toward the sectional, a far more appealing choice than forcing her butt to camp out on a wooden barstool for hours. "Mind if I sit here?"

"Not at all. Wherever you're most comfortable."

She placed the laptops on the ebony coffee table and waited for them to power up while Gavin ground coffee beans. "I need passwords to proceed," she said.

"Yours will work on both laptops."

She logged in, then inserted a drive in each computer to begin the download process. "Weren't Michael and Jane's computers password protected?"

"Those jump drives contain special software that enabled me to bypass their security systems."

"In other words, you hacked into their computers?"

He shrugged. "We do what we need to do to save lives."

"Couldn't you have hacked their computers off-site when you first suspected Michael?"

"We could, but we ran the risk of him realizing his computer had been compromised. We didn't want to take the chance of being discovered early on in the investigation. We had more secure methods of monitoring his online activities.

"Besides, given the information Delta Team had uncovered, we weren't looking at Jane. If your theory is correct, the information we need won't be found on Schuster's computer; we'll find it on hers."

Cassandra wondered what Gavin planned to do regarding Delta Team, but she decided not to broach the subject with him. She doubted he'd tell her, anyway.

"The files are done downloading." Cassandra groaned. "There are thousands of them!" They'd need days to wade through all that data.

Gavin carried over two large steaming mugs, handing one to her as he joined her on the couch. "Good thing I have plenty of Kona beans."

Cassandra settled back against one of the sofa's many patterned throw pillows, the only nod to color in the otherwise black and white apartment. She placed one pillow across her thighs to serve as a makeshift desk.

While Gavin worked his way through Jane's files, she tackled Michael's. "Begin searching with our program of standard keywords," said Gavin. "If nothing pops, work your way through oddly labeled files next."

By two in the morning nothing had popped for either of them. Cassandra began searching through files with names that gave no clue as to their contents. The words on the screen began playing leapfrog over one another, and her brain refused to focus. She kept reading the same sentences over and over. The caffeine-packed Kona no longer worked its magic. She leaned back and closed her eyes to rest them for a few minutes.

~*~

Gavin wondered if someone was playing them. Jane's computer contained nothing but work-related files, mostly psychological questionnaires and reports on patients in various drug studies being conducted by Glenmeade Pharmaceuticals. Were both Schuster and his wife patsies meant to lure him and his teams into a wild goose chase, diverting their attention while the real terrorists carried out their mission? Given the lack of evidence they'd uncovered, the possibility grew more and more likely.

However, that didn't explain Schuster's large purchases of bomb-making chemicals, the phony UPS truck in his garage, or the wife with a possible fake identity—not to mention a possible fake marriage and pregnancy. Nothing added up. What the hell were they missing? And where else could they search to find it?

He decided to go downstairs to check on the facial recognition software program. Noreen had started it running hours ago. Maybe by now they'd have a hit. "I'll be right back," he said.

When Cassandra didn't acknowledge him, Gavin realized she'd fallen asleep. Unlike him, Cassandra wasn't a warrior trained to go for days without sleep. Adrenalin and caffeine only went so far. Still, she'd surpassed his expectation.

He smiled in admiration as he removed the computer from her lap and placed it on the coffee table. Then he tossed aside the pillow and lifted her into his arms. She snuggled into his chest as he carried her to the bedroom, and his body responded in much the same way as it had that first day at target practice.

Years had passed since any woman had aroused him so instantly and with so much intensity. That woman was long dead, and Gavin hadn't thought any other woman would ever move him the way she had. Certainly, none of his brief affairs since had stirred anything close to passion in him. Were the universe and his body trying to tell him something about Cassandra Davenport?

He pushed the thought from his mind and deposited her on his bed. Then he removed her shoes and drew a blanket over her. Before heading downstairs, he stopped in the bathroom and splashed cold water over his face, which proved an unsuccessful substitute for the cold shower he really needed.

Gavin discovered the facial recognition software still running, sifting through hundreds of thousands of images in the database.

Not a single hit had popped up so far.

Instead of returning upstairs, he headed down to the basement and took his frustrations out on a couple of dozen paper targets. Half an hour later he checked the software once more before returning to the apartment.

They had a hit.

TWELVE

Cassandra woke to find herself in Gavin's bed with no idea how she wound up there. She rolled onto her side. The other half of the bed hadn't been disturbed. The alarm clock on the nightstand read 3:05. Hearing no sounds coming from anywhere else in the apartment, she slipped off the bed and padded into the living room. Gavin was nowhere in sight.

The hour-long catnap had revived her enough that her eyes no longer refused to stay open, and her brain no longer felt like mashed potatoes. She poured herself another cup of coffee from the pot on the counter and nuked it in the microwave to warm it up. Then she settled back on the sofa and continued her search through Michael's files.

She'd progressed to the M's in the queue of odd-labeled file names. Clicking on MDSKED brought up a spreadsheet with hundreds of surnames in one column and corresponding abbreviations in a second column. Twenty-five random surnames were highlighted. Cassandra studied the spreadsheet. All the highlighted surnames contained the same abbreviation next to them, THPM.

One by one, she read down the list of all the surnames. None stood out as familiar, but she hardly expected them to, given none included first names. All fell into a variety of ethnicities—everything from O'Hara to Goldberg to Patel to Brown to Markovic. The highlighted names also contained an ethnic mix. As far as she could tell, nothing tied the twenty-five names together other than having the same abbreviation next to them, but that particular abbreviation was also attached to many of the non-highlighted names.

However, when she gave up on the surnames and concentrated her attention on the abbreviations, she immediately zeroed in on something she hadn't first noticed. All of the abbreviations ended with either an AM or a PM.

Morning and afternoon? She scanned down the list of names. There were only ten different abbreviations connected to the hundreds of names. The initials preceding AM and PM confirmed her theory—MO, TU, WE, TH, and FR. Monday, Tuesday, Wednesday, Thursday, and Friday. Obviously, a schedule of some sort. Was this a list of targeted individuals?

Cassandra tried to get into Michael's head. Given the UPS truck, it seemed likely that he and Jane planned an attack using multiple bombs rather than one large bomb. The spreadsheet seemed to confirm this.

And then it hit her. She knew their plan.

Before she had time to verify her hunch, the apartment door opened. "Good, you're awake," said Gavin. "I know who Jane is."

"And I think I know their target," said Cassandra.

"You first," they both said at once.

"No, you," said Cassandra. "I first need to verify."

Gavin handed her a printout of a twelve-year-old Pakistani passport. The picture showed a much younger Jane Smith listed as Rafeeqa Changwani. "She's the daughter of a known Al Qaeda leader killed in a U.S. drone strike five years ago," he said.

Cassandra stared at the photo. "She's out to avenge her father's death."

"Looks that way. What did you discover?"

"First, tell me a bit more about this TATP bomb. Could it take out an entire building?"

Gavin lowered himself onto the coffee table in front of her. "It would depend on the size of the building and the layout, but with enough explosives and positioned properly, the results could be catastrophic."

"So they'd have to place the bombs in strategic locations within a building?"

"For maximum impact, yes."

"That would rule out any building that houses only one company. All packages would be delivered directly to a mailroom for mail clerks to distribute to individual recipients. In most companies if the addressee is someone not working that day, the mailroom would hold onto the package, right?"

"Most likely."

"I think for that reason we can rule out schools, hospitals, pharmaceutical companies, utility companies, and manufacturing facilities. I'd also rule out high-rise apartment complexes because they'd probably have doormen and package lockers, at least the ones they'd target. I doubt they'd bother with moderate or low-income housing."

"So we're looking at a mall, an office park, or a multi-story building that houses many different companies," said Gavin. "I suppose that narrows the targets down somewhat, but we're still left with hundreds of possibilities within a ten-mile radius. Go beyond that, and the numbers increase exponentially."

"I don't think so." Cassandra showed him the spreadsheet. "See the file name?"

"MDSKED?"

"I think MD stands for doctors and SKED for schedule. Michael never could spell. We're looking for a large medical arts building, and if I'm correct, none of these doctors have office hours on Thursday afternoons."

Gavin simultaneously reached for his laptop and the television remote. He turned on the TV, then with a few keystrokes he accessed the MAC server and the data from Michael's phone. "We need to cross-reference those names against the appointments in his calendar. That should give us the location."

"I was about to do that."

Gavin split the TV screen and added the spreadsheet from Cassandra's laptop alongside the phone data. A few more keystrokes and a program began running to compare the information from both files.

"If the packages are addressed directly to individual doctors," said Gavin, "the office managers and receptionists will place the packages on the doctors' desks. No one will discover the bombs ahead of time and alert authorities."

Cassandra nodded. "Once Michael and phony Jane are safely out of the area, they'll remotely detonate the bombs all at once."

The program finished running. "Nice work," said Gavin. A list of names that appeared on both files now filled a third screen.

Cassandra stared at the list. "Those are the twenty-five

highlighted names."

"We've got them," said Gavin. "All of those doctors have offices in the same facility. They're targeting the Medical Arts Building at University Hospital."

Cassandra gasped. "That's a densely populated area, and the building is directly connected to the hospital. If those bombs go off, the collateral damage will be extensive."

"Which is why they chose that location. But now that we know their target, we'll be able to stop them in plenty of time."

"Plenty?" Cassandra worried her bottom lip. "Today is Thursday. We know the truck is ready. They're going to execute their plan today. We might have as little as eight hours to stop them, and we still don't know where they've stashed the bombs."

"You're forgetting, we have tracking devices on both the truck and Changwani's car. They won't be able to deliver the packages until the offices open later this morning. Once they load the bombs in the truck, the good guys will swoop in and arrest them."

So much could still go wrong, but Cassandra tried to banish those thoughts from her brain. "What do you want me to do?"

"Call Noreen and Hanna. Tell them to get in here ASAP. I'm betting that truck is going to leave their garage before daybreak to avoid the possibility of any neighbors seeing them. I'll alert Carla and Tony. It's time to call in the cavalry."

~*~

Within half an hour Homeland Security, the FBI, ATF, and various county bomb squads were mobilized and standing ready. Even though the operation had been handed over to the government, including the monitoring of both the cloned phone and the vehicle tracking devices, Noreen and Hanna continued their own monitoring from a bank of consoles at MAC headquarters.

"Isn't this redundant?" asked Cassandra.

"I'm not willing to risk a government SNAFU that allows Schuster and Changwani to either succeed in their mission or avoid capture," said Gavin. Then he added, "You're with me. We're going to shadow that truck in case things go awry and we need someone other than an agency operative to talk down Schuster."

She snorted. "He never listened to me while we were married. What makes you think he'd listen to me now?"

"He probably won't, but we have to keep all options open."

"They're awake," said Noreen. "Sounds like they're getting ready to head out."

"Let's go," said Gavin.

He and Cassandra headed for the elevator, but instead of pushing the button for the garage, Gavin pushed the button for the basement. When the doors opened, he headed for the firing range. Cassandra followed a step behind him.

Gavin retrieved a Glock and two clips from the weapons locker. He inserted one clip into the gun, then turned to face her. Their eyes locked. "I need to know I can count on you," he said.

Cassandra nodded and held out her hand. Her personal feelings about guns no longer mattered. Chances were slim she'd become the last line of defense in stopping her madman ex-husband and his Al Qaeda wife, but she was prepared to do whatever it took to prevent them from succeeding. "You can."

Gavin placed the gun and extra clip in her hand, and they continued to the garage.

Noreen and Hanna kept them apprised of the two vehicles as they tracked their whereabouts. Both the car and the truck drove from the house in Millburn to a strip mall in Springfield where they left the car. The UPS truck continued on down Morris Avenue. From conversation Noreen picked up, they knew both Michael and his Pakistani bride were on board.

"They plan to ditch the truck in the strip mall parking lot afterwards and take off in the car," said Cassandra.

"Don't worry," said Gavin. "They'll never get that far with their plan."

She wished she could be as positive. The government had thwarted many terrorist attacks since 9/11 but not all of them. Were the odds in their favor or stacked against them?

~*~

Twenty minutes later, the UPS truck pulled into a warehouse complex off the Turnpike in Port Elizabeth. Gavin and Cassandra followed two minutes later.

Once inside the complex, Gavin killed the lights and slowly drove down the street, turning into a trucking company parking lot. Across the road a UPS truck sat at a loading dock. He handed Cassandra a pair of night vision binoculars. The two of them watched as three men carefully loaded cartons one at a time from the warehouse into the truck.

"Did Delta Team ever follow Michael to any of those doctor appointments he listed in his calendar?" she asked.

"They were supposed to follow him everywhere once they discovered the chemical purchases. Why?"

"I don't think they did."

"What are you suggesting?"

"Those weren't doctor appointments in his calendar. Look at the name above the warehouse. DR Wholesale and Distribution."

"Shit!"

Delta Team had a lot to answer for, and Cassandra couldn't help but take a small amount of pleasure in that fact after the way they'd tried to blame her for their own screw-ups.

"They're toast," Noreen whispered. Cassandra hazarded a quick glance at Gavin. He, too, had heard Noreen. In the dim light she could see the tight set of his mouth.

"We'll discuss this later," he said.

Michael, dressed in a UPS uniform, stepped out of the truck to stand alongside it while the men continued to load boxes. "I don't see Jane—Chang-whatever," she said.

"She's probably inside directing the loading."

Cassandra swept the binoculars to the left and right of the warehouse. "Where are all the good guys who are supposed to stop this?"

"Hiding in plain sight," said Gavin. "Like us. Once the truck is completely loaded, they'll swoop in and make the arrests. They want all the bombs in one small, contained location first."

"There's no chance of any detonating?"

"Not by them. We've jammed their phones, but TATP is very unstable. Something could still go wrong."

An image of Cooper and Hayley flashed before Cassandra's mind. No matter how large a salary Gavin paid her, all the money in the world wouldn't be worth leaving her kids orphaned. "Are we far enough away if something does go wrong?"

"Probably."

She scowled at him. "You need to learn to sugarcoat the truth better."

"I'll work on it."

A few minutes passed as the men continued the loading process. When the last box had been placed inside the truck, one of the men pulled down the overhead door at the back of the truck and secured the latch.

Jane stepped from inside the warehouse and joined Michael at the side of the truck. She, too, wore a UPS uniform. A moment later a shot rang out, and Michael fell to the ground.

Cassandra gasped. "She shot him!"

Jane stepped into the truck and started the engine while one of the men from the loading dock dragged Michael's body into the shadows.

As Jane navigated down the driveway toward the street, dozens of government vehicles, their lights flashing and their sirens blaring, approached from multiple directions, blocking her escape. Overhead three helicopters suddenly appeared and hovered above, their rotors stirring up the dirt and gravel, spotlights aimed at the truck.

Jane gunned the engine, then rammed the truck into the vehicle directly in front of her. A moment later a shot rang out from the roof of one of the adjacent buildings, and she collapsed over the steering wheel.

THIRTEEN

Before returning to MAC headquarters Gavin stopped at an all-night diner in Elizabeth. The smell of frying bacon filled the air. Cassandra's stomach immediately growled. "Hungry?" he asked.

She glanced at the clock on the wall above the counter. "Aside from your Kona, I haven't had anything in my stomach in more than twelve hours."

"That makes two of us." He glanced around the room "The food must be good here. The place is packed with truckers."

They settled into one of the few unoccupied booths, took one look at the menu, and decided on the breakfast special—three eggs, bacon, home fries, and a short stack of pancakes.

After the waitress brought coffee, Gavin raised his mug to her. "Here's to Cassandra Davenport, the best decision I've made since agreeing to head up one of the satellite facilities."

She clinked her mug against his. Gavin grinned at her, his eyes twinkling. A flutter skipped around in her stomach, and she felt a flush course up her neck and into her cheeks. She lowered her head, bit her bottom lip, and stared into her coffee.

He reached for her hand. "Tell me if I'm out of line here, but you feel it, too, don't you?"

She nodded, leaving her hand in his, and raised her head. "What do we do about it?"

"I don't know. Mixing business and pleasure is usually a recipe for disaster, especially in our line of work."

"I suppose." She started to withdraw her hand, but he held fast.

"However, it has worked for others."

"What others?"

"Carla Jordan used to have a hard and fast rule, no fraternizing among the troops."

"What happened?"

"Her operatives started falling in love with each other."

"How did she handle it?"

Gavin shrugged. "She gave in to the inevitable. She'd been in love with her second-in-command for years and him with her, but they both kept their feelings bottled up."

"It's never a good idea to keep feelings bottled up," said Cassandra. "It makes you sick."

"True." They sat holding hands and smiling at each other until their breakfast arrived.

~*~

Later that afternoon Cassandra stood over Michael's hospital bed, staring down in disgust at her ex. A myriad of machines whirred and beeped around him. One of his arms contained an IV. A pair of handcuffs circled his other wrist and attached to the bedrail. "Is he unconscious?"

"No, just heavily sedated," said Gavin, "but according to Tony, he blurted out everything, hoping to cut a deal, before they wheeled him into surgery."

Cassandra's jaw dropped. "He wasn't offered a deal, was he?"

"No way. Changwani is dead, her cohorts from the warehouse rounded up and locked up. Schuster had nothing of substance to offer the Feds. He was played by a terrorist who tricked him into marrying her, then manipulated him to aid her in her plan. The fool didn't even know she wasn't really pregnant."

Cassandra rolled her eyes. "I can believe that. Once I started showing, he didn't want to have anything to do with me."

Gavin grunted.

"I still find it hard to believe he planned to murder so many innocent people."

"He did it for the money," said Gavin. "You were right about that. She promised him two million dollars. We found their passports and airline tickets in the trunk of her car."

"Where were they headed?"

"Caracas. Of course, she never planned to take him with her."

"There's no fool like a greedy, blind fool."

Gavin wrapped his arm around her shoulders. "Revenge was a powerful motive for him, as well."

"How so?"

"He said most of the doctors he dealt with treated him like a second-class citizen. He decided to teach them a lesson."

"He was always jealous of anyone richer or more successful, especially doctors. Is that why they chose to bomb a building full of medical offices?"

"He chose the target. Changwani didn't care what they blew up as long as they took out hundreds of lives."

Cassandra leaned her head on Gavin's shoulder. "Even if he'd gotten into med school, he would have made a lousy doctor. He never cared about anyone but himself."

As Gavin led her from the room, she said, "I only have one regret."

"That you didn't pull the trigger?"

"No, I'm quite comfortable with not having done that."

"Then what?"

"I'll never have the satisfaction of being able to tell him I was the person who brought him down."

Gavin laughed. "Unfortunately, that's the one downside of this job."

ABOUT THE AUTHOR

USA Today and Amazon bestselling and award-winning author Lois Winston writes mystery, romance, romantic suspense, chick lit, women's fiction, children's chapter books, and nonfiction under her own name and her Emma Carlyle pen name. *Kirkus Reviews* dubbed her critically acclaimed Anastasia Pollack Crafting Mystery series, "North Jersey's more mature answer to Stephanie Plum." In addition, Lois is an award-winning craft and needlework designer who often draws much of her source material for both her characters and plots from her experiences in the crafts industry. Learn more about Lois and her books, where to find her on social media, and a link for signing up for her newsletter at www.loiswinston.com.